SHAOLINA

Maha Al Fahim

Maha Publishing • Vancouver, Canada

Ebook ISBN 978-0-9917576-4-0
Softcover ISBN 978-0-9917576-3-3

Publisher's Cataloging-in-Publication Data

Al Fahim, Maha, 1997-, author.
Shaolina / Maha Al Fahim.
Vancouver, BC: Maha Publishing, 2020.
978-0-9917576-3-3 (pbk.) | 978-0-9917576-4-0 (ebook)
LCSH Shao lin si (Dengfeng Xian, China)—Fiction. | Martial arts—
China—Fiction. | Kung fu—Fiction. | Motion pictures—United
States—Fiction. | Motion picture industry—United States—Fiction.
| China—Civilization—Fiction. Women—China—Fiction. | Com-
ing of age—Fiction. | Fame—Fiction. |Hollywood (Los Angeles,
Calif.)—Fiction. | BISAC FICTION/ General
LCC PS3601.L35965 S53 2020 | DDC 813.6—dc23

Published by Maha Publishing
Vancouver, BC, Canada

Cover Design – Linda Parke (www.ravenbookdesign)
Interior Design – Toni Serofin (www.sanserofin.com)

First Printing April 2020
Printed and bound in Canada

ACKNOWLEDGEMENT

To my parents; thank you for all your love and consistent support. Through your example, you have taught me to work hard, and to view happiness not as the meaning of life, but as the byproduct of a meaningful life.

To my sister, Fatima, and brother, Mohamed; thank you for your unwavering energy, enthusiasm and encouragement. I am very lucky to have you as my siblings and friends.

I am also grateful to the monks at the Shaolin Temple and surrounding Kung Fu schools. Thank you for warmly welcoming me to training and for sharing your personal experiences. You have shown me the beauty of cultivating one's potential.

PROLOGUE

Sometimes, we sleepwalk through life, and only when we are about to die do we truly awaken.

With the gun pressed to her head, Li felt the fog in her mind lift. She saw with clarity the person she had become. She felt as though an ocean were deluging the chambers of her heart, drowning her. She was sinking to the bottom. She gasped, she fought, she tried to surface. *If only I could—.* Like stinging saltwater, regret clawed up the back of her throat, choking her. She was not ready to die. Tears were streaming down her cheeks, as though the salt in her throat had found an outlet through her eyes. But she could not weep out the ocean inside. *If only I could turn back time.*

CHAPTER 1

Twenty-five years earlier. A small village in Henan Province, China.

Dusk was descending, and the last of the Asian koels were flocking into the pink and golden sky, releasing their siren-like calls. But Hai remained in the cornfield. A farmer in his early twenties, he had a small, raw-boned stature, a long face, and tanned skin.

With a hoe in hand, he brushed the soil to and fro, preparing the earth for planting. The rhythmic movement of the act let his mind wander. Any day now, his pregnant wife would give birth. It had to be a boy this time. He had already chosen a name for him. He imagined a son standing next to him in this field, helping him till the land and pick the harvests. No, he shook his head, he would send their boy to school, to become educated and get a good job in the city.

Hai rested, leaning on his hoe and gazing into the distance. An autumn breeze brushed sweat from his forehead.

The thought of walking his son to school every morning, and boasting of him in front of the villagers, raised a tickle of anticipation in his stomach. As he held the hoe again, his thumb felt light, like the tool could slip from his fingers any second.

He went back to brushing the soil. Yes, this would be the pride of his family. He would show off not only to the villagers but also to his elder brother, and village official, Feng. *Feng.* He would show him, that swindler and liar. His grip around the hoe suddenly hardened.

"HAI!" A cry echoed across the field, snapping him from his thoughts.

"HAI!" came the voice again.

Hai rested his hoe and turned to check whether his ears were playing tricks on him.

In the darkening purple sky, the silhouette of a man came running towards him. As the silhouette drew closer, Hai realized it was his neighbor. "Your wife—," the man spoke between gasps. "Your wife's about to give birth! Hurry!"

Hai's heartbeat quickened, and his hoe dropped. As he ran towards his house, excitement, fear, and nervousness churned within. His thoughts chased after him, then raced by faster than he could run. He flung open the light wooden door and suddenly heard a baby's cry.

"What *is it*? What *is it*?" he asked.

There was no response. Even the baby's cries stopped. Hai could now hear the kitchen sink tap dripping into a clay bowl nearly filled with water: *tick, tick*. He looked to the thatched roof. A moth was hovering about the yellow light bulb. Returning his gaze downward, he saw his three-year-old daughter, Mei; frightened, she was clenching her doll against her chest. She looked up at him with mahogany brown eyes. Her nervous energy began to seep into him.

Suddenly, the tattered dark green curtains that separated the living room from the bedroom were pulled aside, and an elderly midwife appeared. She cradled the baby, wrapped in white cloth. Its eyes were closed, its skin soft and pale. Hai tried to glean the baby's gender from the midwife's expression, but her heavily wrinkled face betrayed neither joy nor disappointment. He glanced past the curtains to his wife, Lian. Looking pallid against the bedclothes, she tried to avoid his eyes. More nervous now, he returned his attention to the midwife.

"*Well?*" he asked impatiently.

The midwife looked at Hai's face, his eager, anxious expression. Unable to meet his eyes, she looked at the baby, then placed it in Hai's arms. "You have another girl," she said in a frail voice.

At that moment, the moth hovering above hit the searing light bulb and plunged to the ground. As the moth's wings burned, so did the hopes and dreams in Hai's heart. Though the baby was light, his knees buckled under her weight.

He stared blankly, darkness engulfing his surroundings and bitterness gnawing at his heart. He swallowed, fighting a rising lump in his throat, but he could not quell the liquid blurring his eyes. His brother, Feng, had everything—his parents' favor, power as a village official, and the respect of the villagers—even though he had stolen Hai's land rights. Now, while Feng had a son able to continue his family lineage, Hai would continue to be the weak one with daughters.

Two hard knocks sounded suddenly on the door. At the third knock, the door itself gave way and opened. To Hai's surprise, standing in the doorway, with his belly protruding, was Feng.

As he saw Hai carrying the baby with a somber expression, a smile began creeping across Feng's face. He quickly tried to conceal it, saying, "I was walking nearby when I heard your wife gave birth!"

Hai gazed at his brother's gleaming black eyes.

"What did she bring?"

Hai felt himself standing on the edge of a rocky cliff, one word separating a life at the top from a fall to the bottom.

"*Hmmm?*" Feng pressed.

The rocks beneath him seemed to quiver, and his body quaked. He gazed down the cliff and saw a void of bottomless blackness. "Father of girls," "weak family," "cursed," "*duanzi juesun,*" echoed back at him. A man needed a son to care for him in his twilight years and to raise the strength and status of his family. As Confucian culture dictated, he also needed a son to continue his lineage. *Duanzi juesun*—to die sonless, ending the family line—was the worst destiny to befall someone.

4

When the villagers quarreled, it was among the gravest curses they could wish on an opponent. Looking into the void, Hai foresaw this life of greater hardship and humiliation. Every passing second seemed to tow him closer and closer to it.

No. He straightened his spine. He would not surrender to such a life. Slowly, Hai looked up, glaring into his brother's eyes.

"I have a *son*," he said.

Feng's eyes flew wide with surprise, and his mask of affability dissolved.

"Congratulations," he found his voice. "I am happy for you. You have a ward to help you in your farm work." Then he turned and left.

At the sound of the door slamming, a sneering smile tugged on Hai's lips. From rocky ground, he managed to lift himself to solid foundations. But the smile was ephemeral.

"Hai what did you do?" his wife called in panic from the bedroom. "We can't live our whole lives keeping up this lie!"

Hai rushed to the bedroom, placed the baby on his wife's lap, and flung out his arms. "This is your fault! Had you borne me a son, we would have no need for a lie!"

The baby stirred and let out an uncomfortable cry, aggravating the tension between them. Mei peeked from the doorway, staring at her parents, and the midwife hurriedly entered. She took the baby from Lian's lap and rocked her gently. "Sh-sh-sh," she whispered.

And the baby, feeling her warmth and assurance, quieted.

The midwife paced to Hai and showed him the baby. "Look at her forehead—the width, the height. She is a lucky one. She is destined for a life of fortune."

"He is lucky, *he*," Hai corrected her. He sighed then faced her. "Promise me one thing, elder... Don't tell anyone her true identity. Please."

"Your task of maintaining this story will be difficult," the midwife slowly began. "But mine of keeping quiet is easy. You have my promise."

His chest a little lighter, Hai paced to a window hole. He raised his head, as though trying to look at something in the distance, over the hills. But the darkness of the night limited how far he could see.

"What will you name him?" the midwife spoke after a long silence.

He took a deep breath and faced her. "We will name him Lì."

CHAPTER 2

Hiding someone's identity is like hiding the sun behind a hill. At dawn, when its head is low and its light is dim, any hill can hide it. But as it rises and grows, no mountain is large enough to reach its height, nor wide enough to absorb its light. Then, brilliantly it shines, burning the eyes of those who thought otherwise.

During Li's first few years, hiding her identity was manageable. Hai boasted to the villagers that he had a son, while resting assured that Li was at home, away from their sight. But as Li grew, Hai had plans to send her to school, so she would become cultured and educated, like his brother's son, find better job prospects in the city, and bring back more wealth and status to the family. With such grand dreams came risk. Hai felt this as the now six-year-old Li prepared for her first day of school.

Lian dressed her in a fresh, white shirt and gave her a glossy blue backpack. "Whoaaw," Li let out as she took the bag. She unzipped it, then inhaled the smell of new plastic. It brought a tingling to her stomach and made her excited to begin school. She then noticed the fresh notebook and new pencil case inside. Unzipping the latter, she found an array of pencil crayons, a pencil sharpener, and an eraser. Mei looked over Li's shoulder at the treasure trove of stationery.

"I want to go to school!" she yelled.

"Trust me, Mei," Lian's voice was gentle, "you will learn much more useful things for your life here, at home." It was too expensive to send both Li and Mei to school, with all the books, materials, and other miscellaneous fees.

Mei pouted. "But I also want to learn school stuff!"

Lian pursed her lips in thought, then turned away from her. "Li, how many ears do you have?"

"Two," Li said, touching them, as though to make sure they were still there.

Lian then gently held Mei's ears and made a show of transferring them onto Li's head. "Well, now you have four ears. You will listen for yourself as well as for your sister. When you come back home, you can teach her what you learned."

Slightly mollified, Mei nodded in approval.

"Okay?" Lian said.

"Okay," Li giggled.

"Where is the cap I bought for him?" Hai interrupted, searching through the house.

A white baseball cap on top of their mint-green cabinet caught his eye. "Ah!" He grabbed it and came to place it firmly on Li's head.

"You want to hide him even more?" Zhi Rou asked,

exasperated. "Already you shave his head so much, I no longer know what color his hair is."

"It's for the sun, it's for the sun," Hai muttered, bothered by her teasing.

Grabbing her packed lunch and backpack from her mother, Li returned to her father's side. Hai grasped her hand and took a deep breath, filling his chest with air and lifting his face into a smile. They set out.

As they crossed the village, they passed by men grinding wheat and walking oxen, and women hanging clothes to dry. Hai beamed as he felt them look up from their work at him and Li.

An older villager carrying a basket of grains over his head was walking by.

"Good morning," Hai said as the villager looked at them. "This is Li. I am walking him to school."

"Ah! Your boy has grown!" The villager's face lit up. "Let me see him, let me see him." He put down his basket and trotted over to Li, bending down to get a closer view of her.

Li looked up to meet his gaze from under her brim. The cap now framed her plum cheeks and round face and hid her shaved head. Hai glanced at her and was alarmed to find that she looked more like a sweet girl wearing a cap than a boy.

The old man stared fixedly at Li. A hesitant laugh escaped Hai. His grip on Li's hand tightened.

Still, the old man neither stirred nor uttered a single word.

Fear spiked in Hai. *What if he's onto me? What if he has already figured out Li's true identity, that this is all a ruse?* The palpitations of his heart quickened. Still the man's dark eyes examined Li.

"Hai!" the old man yelled. Hai stiffened. "Your son is handsome!"

As the old man patted him on the back, Hai's heart seemed to spring from his chest.

When the villager continued on his way, Hai quickly removed Li's cap.

"Why?" Li asked.

"Your mother is right. You don't need it."

When they arrived at the red-brick schoolhouse, Hai saw a man standing nearby.

"Excuse me, I'm here with my son," he said. "Where is the class for the first grade?"

"Go down this corridor," the doorman gestured, "and it's the second room on the left."

"Thank you."

As he followed the directions and entered the class, he found they were the first ones there. In his eagerness, he had come too early. Never mind, he would stand and look around the room. He gazed up at the string of Chinese characters pasted along the gray walls. Facing the black chalkboard were rows of wooden desks. And sitting in the front row, eagerly, was Li.

"Oh no, no," Hai quickly admonished. "You can't sit here. You'll be too close to the teacher." He grabbed her hand and led her to a row in the back, farthest away from the teacher's desk. He could not afford another close call.

Li tugged her hand back, halting him. "No, I don't want to sit at the back. I need to listen well to the teacher. I'll be listening for Mei too." The two went back and forth until finally, he relented. She could sit in the second row, but at the far end.

When other students began trickling into the room, he said goodbye. As he walked back to the field, the thought that someone might discover Li's true identity tormented him.

At school, the teacher arrived—a middle-aged man dressed in a black robe, with a mop of black hair, bushy brows, and a mole on his nose. Upon seeing him, Li sat upright. She was ready to embed into her mind, and transfer to Mei, anything and everything she learned.

But as the teacher droned on, she found that she barely understood him. *Was he from a different village?*

She leaned closer, struggling to pick up on what he was saying, but his voice faded into the background, and Li could only see his mouth moving.

Soon, her eyes began to droop. To stop her head from following, she propped it on her palm. But gradually, her hand gave way, and she melted into a puddle on her desk.

"*Whack!!!*" A loud sound right next to her ear made her shoot upright in the seat. She looked up to find the teacher, cross, holding a large ruler.

"Are you here in my class to nap?!" he yelled.

At the sight of his beady, angry gaze, her throat went dry. She could only stare open-eyed.

"If you cannot pay attention, then move to the back! Let someone more deserving sit here. *Yuzhong!*" he called a boy from the back. "Come here." He pointed to Li's desk.

Li was miserable. Her legs felt heavy as she picked up her books and walked to the back, passing the sneering eyes and sniggers of the other kids.

A few minutes later, the bell rang, beckoning them to break time. The students flooded out from the cool, dark classroom onto the sunbaked fields. The older boys were playing ball, while others were scattered around, watching them.

Li found a spot under the shade of a large tree. She sat, leaning against its trunk, then pulled her lunch from her bag. As she ate a mouthful of her rice, she gazed at the kids playing on the dirt field, their screams and chatter filling the air. Lunch was difficult to swallow. This school day was harder than she'd expected. As she continued slowly eating, a few grains of rice dropped onto the ground. An ant crawled by, hoisted a grain, and tried to carry it on its back. Almost immediately, another ant came and helped carry the piece of rice. Li looked down at the miniature scene unfolding before her. It brought a smile to her face that these ants now had food to take back to their families.

She dropped another grain of rice, watching with fascination now as more ants gathered.

Suddenly, at the sound of a bell ringing, students stampeded towards the door. One of them stepped on some of the ants, leaving them crippled.

"Hey!" Crimson rushed to Li's face. She waved her fist after the boy. "You stepped on my—" she started but trailed off as she realized the boy was already gone.

"Class is starting!" the teacher yelled.

Li groaned as she picked up her bag and headed back to the dark classroom. The teacher gave them arithmetic and calligraphy homework at the end of the school day. He threatened a beating with the large ruler for those who did not do their homework. Li mentally prepared a story to tell her family why she did not want to go to school anymore. She rehearsed this story as she walked with a stream of students down the corridor and out the school door.

Hai was standing outside, waiting. His palms were damp with worry. Had anyone questioned Li's identity? As soon as he saw Li walk out the door alongside the other boys, his fears subsided and were replaced with pride.

Li saw her father standing in the distance, a smile on his face as she approached. "How was school?!" he asked in a voice full of enthusiasm.

"Uhh…" She looked again at his bright face. "It was good," she muttered.

Hai took her backpack and grasped her hand. On their way back, he enthused about the status she would bring to the family, and how he could not wait until the day she graduated. He could boast to all the villagers. Li kept her gaze on the ground, wondering how she would begin to tell her family that she did not want to go to school tomorrow.

While they walked the same path home, each followed their own line of thought, but both were so absorbed that the journey was quick. Soon they were facing their mud house.

As Hai opened the door, the smell of fried noodles poured from the house and wafted over Li. Her mother was stirring food on the stove while Mei was setting plates on the table.

As Mei's eyes caught Li's, they filled with excitement. She ran to grab a pencil and paper and rushed to Li. "Teach me! Teach me what you learned today!"

"Mei!" her mother scolded. "Li just came back! Let her rest!" She then turned to Li. "I made your favorite food. Come, come, sit, eat." She sat Li at the table.

Li looked from her mother to Mei to her father. Seeing their large smiles and joyous energy, her rehearsed story of quitting school dissolved.

CHAPTER 3

With the passage of time, Li became accustomed to her teacher's dialect and picked up more and more vocabulary. When she came home, she would often make a classroom under the dinner table with Mei. A plank of wood served as their chalkboard, and she collected whatever bits of chalk the teacher tossed on the ground, bringing them home for teaching her sister.

One evening, the family was sitting around the dinner table, a naked bulb spreading a dim glow upon them. Li stirred her soup. "I saw something strange at school today," she began.

Hai's eyes widened while he gulped a spoonful of soup.

It had been break time. The boys were playing soccer on the sunbaked dirt field, and, as usual, Li was standing on the sidelines, eating her lunch while watching them.

One of the boys suddenly kicked the ball so high that it flew over the bushes and disappeared. The team captain turned to Li. "Go get it!" he yelled.

Startled, but delighted at the chance to take part in the game, Li skipped into a sprint after the ball. She found it lying in tangled bush branches. As she reached to reclaim it from the branches' grasp, something caught her eyes.

Just beyond, on a tree by the river, a boy was pissing. It was not the pissing that alarmed her but the flesh between his legs. It was stick–like, and Li could only stare. *Why is he different from me?* she wondered. *Is he ill?*

The pissing boy caught her gaze. "Hey!" he yelled. "What are you looking at?"

Quickly, Li had grabbed the ball, scrambled to her feet, and run back to the open field.

Li and Mei both laughed at the story, but Hai began choking on his soup.

"Oh dear!" Lian stood up.

Hai waved his hand as though to say, "I'm fine, I'm fine." But tears formed at the edges of his eyes.

Lian took his arm and led him to their room. Li and Mei now grew quiet, wondering why their parents were acting strangely.

Once inside, Lian pulled their curtain closed behind her. "The time has come that you must tell her," she said in a whisper.

Hai sat on the edge of their bed and shook his head. "It's too early, it's too early."

"She is old enough now, she must know," Lian said as she joined him on the bed's edge, facing him.

Hai looked down. "I'm afraid that she's too young to keep a secret."

"I know Li. She has a curious nature. If you don't tell her now, she'll search for an explanation of what she saw. And that could expose her identity."

Hai kept his head down, uncertain.

"The best way to keep the secret safe is to tell her."

Gradually, Hai lifted his gaze, meeting Lian's eyes. She nodded. In a last-ditch effort, he said, "Don't you think we can wait a little longer?"

She shook her head.

He sighed.

Lian rose from the bed. "Leave it to me. I can tell her." Never enthusiastic about this ruse from the beginning, she was ready to bring one part of it to an end. Sliding the curtain aside, she found Li and Mei still at the table, now playing with pomegranate seeds. They were lining them up on the wooden surface to form shapes.

As the parents returned to their seats, Li and Mei looked up at them.

"Li, I have something very important to tell you," Lian

began. "But I need your promise that you will keep it a secret."

Li nodded, eager to be in on the secret.

"This secret Mei has known for a while," Lian said while looking to Mei, "and we are grateful that she kept it all this time."

Mei smiled.

Lian then turned to Li. She spoke slowly. "When you were born, Li… You were born a girl. But we raised you as a boy."

Li's mouth opened, but no words came out. At once lost and dumbfounded, she could only stare.

"If a family has no son," Lian began to explain, "it is seen as weak. No one will respect your father. All the villagers will bully and tease him, and his health will suffer." She looked more earnestly at Li now. "You don't want your father's heart to hurt? For him to grow ill?" Li shook her head. "You don't want to lose your father?" Li more quickly and vehemently shook her head. "Because then, we will have no one to support us," Lian concluded.

Hai affected a cough. Li got up from her seat and went to her father, wrapping her arms around his neck. "No, baba," she said, "I love you very much. I won't let anything bad happen to you." As she squeezed her eyes shut, Hai could feel drops of her warm tears on his shirt.

Mei kept her gaze on her lap.

CHAPTER 4

After that day, they never spoke of the matter. But it was incessantly at the forefront of Li's thoughts. Upon learning that she was a girl, Li felt weak and inferior, and afraid that at any second, someone might discover her secret. She was perpetually on her toes, her heart on edge. But with time, she accepted that she had no other option. She had to grow tougher. *Boys are naturally stronger,* her mother's voice rang through her head. *But girls can learn to be just as strong, or even stronger.*

During lunch times, she saw the school ball as a chance to show off her masculinity. She no longer handed it to the players when it flew over the bushes; she kicked it to them. She picked up sticks and aggressively fenced with the other boys, aiming to knock the sticks out of their hands.

She also more closely observed the behavior of other boys, especially the rough ones, and emulated them. She raised her chin. When she walked, she would kick the rocks and empty cans in her way. Though her appetite was small, she would finish her lunch in a few big bites;

when she choked, she would pound on her chest to make the food go down. She spoke foully and, when she did clean her mouth, she wiped it with the edge of her sleeve.

In the span of three years, her position on the school field advanced from watching on the sidelines to keeping goal to playing the field, each time getting closer to the ball. But no matter how much she tried to masculinize her behavior and mannerisms, she had no control over her velvet skin or plum lips, her rosy cheeks or long eyelashes. And as she grew, her feminine features became more prominent, threatening to expose her identity.

This was a concern that continued to hover in Hai's mind as he worked alongside fellow farmers. Other concerns competed for space too. It was spring, and the conditions for farming were especially favorable. He and other farmers worked on Feng's leased land, and Feng would give them a small percentage of the profit on every unit they produced. To make full use of the good weather, Hai worked from sunrise to sunset. He was saving up to build a bigger house now that his children were older and needed more space.

At noon, the farmers took a break. They would sit under the shade of a walnut tree, eat their lunch, and discuss the village gossip. On this particular day, the conversation turned to Hai's older brother.

"I heard he got a lucrative contract with a city hotel," one of the farmers said. "They'll be buying all their pomegranates exclusively from him." He looked at Hai. "They say your former land and your brother's land have the richest soil and grow the sweetest fruits."

Hai fastened his eyes on the farmer, enthralled by every word.

"You did know this already, didn't you?" the farmer looked at Hai.

Hai blinked. "Ah, yes, yes, I did," he lied.

"He will make a lot of money, and your share of his profits will also grow."

"Yes, yes."

As two other farmers continued talking, Hai's mind transported him years into the past.

A few days after Mei had been born, Hai was on his land, tilling the soil. All of the land was state property, but the state allocated to each household in the village land rights for up to thirty years. Feng had approached Hai with an affable demeanor that day. He said that alone, Hai could not be very productive on his land. He did not have the many male workers that Feng had, nor did he have Feng's tractors and other farm tools. But he needed money, especially now that he had a child to look after.

So he suggested that Hai sell him his land rights. Feng promised a generous compensation. And as a bonus, he would let Hai work on his farmland and receive a share of the profits on every unit of crop he produced. It was a great deal, Feng assured him, and he only offered it to help out his brother.

Caught in Feng's magnetic web, and overawed by his stature as a village official, Hai agreed, and when Feng came to him with the legal documents, he willingly signed. Unable to read, he put his faith in his brother's word.

Feng seized the land, but he gave Hai less than a fiftieth of what it was worth. From time to time, Hai approached him, asking for the rest of his promised compensation. But every time, Feng found a means to push him away. It was only a matter of time before Hai realized he had been deceived. But he was too ashamed to admit it. If he revealed his loss, the whole village would view him as a loser. And he was too afraid to challenge Feng—who was both his elder brother and a powerful man in the village.

So he kept silent. He bottled up his rage, and it corroded him like acid. He needed an escape. He needed to run, to shout, to scream at the top of his lungs and let it out.

"Hai? Are you okay?"

Hai snapped out of his thoughts. He found the two farmers looking up at him. Then he noticed that he was on his feet, his fists tightened.

"Oh…" He loosened his fist. "I'm not feeling well. I'm going to go home now."

They nodded, and he left.

As he strode home, every joint in his body complained, every fiber in his neck and back muscles screamed in pain. Here he was, laboring day in and day out to eke out a little of the money his brother had in mounds, from land that should've been partly his.

He squeezed his sore neck, and lightning pain shot through his nerves. "Ach!" he exhaled. Still, this physical pain was nothing compared with his mental anguish. At least with some rest and sleep, the former could heal.

But the latter gave him no rest and plagued him while he tried to sleep.

Arriving, he pushed open his shoddy front door. On the living room floor, nine-year-old Li and twelve-year-old Mei were playing teacher and student. A few dolls were sitting beside them, completing their pretend classroom.

Seeing Li with the dolls, Hai's eyes flew wide with alarm. He erupted at his wife. "Lian! How could you let this happen?!"

Lian, who was busy preparing food, quickly turned. She wiped her hands on her apron as she approached. "What happened? What happened?"

Hai's face turned crimson. He grabbed one of the dolls and ripped its head from its body, then threw both pieces to the floor.

"Reckless fools!" he pointed forcefully at each of them. "Do you know... if they saw... what could've happened?" The possibility of the villagers catching Li playing with dolls fueled the rage he had carried home with him from the fields. Bellowing, he lunged at the remaining dolls and kicked them, one after another.

The girls, never having seen their father this way, backed away against the wall. Hai kept hollering, raging against the dolls, against his brother, against all the injustices of the world. Then suddenly, he felt a snap in his chest. He stopped, stepped backwards, and—

"Oh dear!" Lian ran to catch him before he fell. "Please, take it easy, take it easy. I promise this won't happen again."

Panicking, she slung his arm over her shoulder and helped him to their room. There she lay him on the bed.

Hai kept breathing heavily.

Fearing for her husband, she rushed to grab the mid-wife—the closest thing the village had to a doctor. On her way out of the room, she saw Mei standing and clutching her shirt where her heart was.

Lian forcefully pointed at her. "This is *your* fault! I told you a hundred times before, don't play dolls with Li." Mei's eyes reddened, and her face looked strained, as though she were holding in unbearable pain.

A quarter of an hour later, Lian was back, the midwife in tow. They found Hai asleep.

Mei was now standing closer to him, crying. "Baba, don't die." Li was a few feet further away, staring as though in a daze, her face stricken with fear.

Lian brushed aside the girls as she walked to the bed. The midwife felt Hai's pulse at his wrist. Next, she checked his eyes and tongue. She then turned to Lian. "He will be fine," she said calmly. "He just needs some rest."

The two women stepped away and quietly pulled the bedroom curtain closed behind them. Li and Mei were waiting.

The midwife lay a hand on Mei's arm. "Don't worry," she said, "your father will be fine."

Mei let out a tiny breath of relief.

"But you take care of him."

She nodded earnestly.

Then the midwife stepped towards Li. She scrutinized her but remained silent. Li gave an uncomfortable smile.

"It's getting dark," Lian said. "I will walk you back." She picked up a gas lantern from the shelf.

As the two women headed out, they felt the night breeze and saw the purple sky marked by the silhouettes of sleeping trees.

"It worries me," Lian said in a whisper. "He's been having so many nightmares lately—about the villagers finding out the truth."

"I don't blame him," the midwife said. "Li is looking less and less like a boy."

"I don't know what to do! All this stress is taking a toll on his health."

The midwife looked down at the cool, dark sand beneath their feet. "I have thought about your situation," she said finally. "Why don't you send Li to the Shaolin Temple?"

"The Shaolin Temple?" Lian stopped abruptly, her voice breaking from its whisper.

"Shhhhhh," the midwife placed a finger to her lips. "It would be better for you all," she continued in a whisper. "It would make Li strong. And meanwhile, it would remove her from the prying eyes of the villagers without raising their suspicions."

A chilly evening breeze brushed them.

Lian rubbed both her arms, thinking uncomfortably about it as they resumed walking. Her father had told her stories of the legendary Shaolin Temple. It was considered the birthplace of Chan Buddhism, over a thousand years ago. But it was also where many martial arts styles were combined and systematized, and where Shaolin Kung Fu had been born. The temple took in boys as young as three years old—some orphans and others sent by their parents for various reasons—making disciples and warriors out of them. Her father said the temple's combination of spirituality and martial arts was potent. The monks' intense training of both mind and body helped them withstand pain and perform seemingly superhuman feats.

Lian at times saw some of the younger monks in the village market. They wore shaved heads, orange robes, and radiant expressions. They walked nimbly, snaking through the streets, sometimes carrying a watermelon or two. But Lian knew their lean appearances were deceptive. Some could run along walls and move with impossible agility. Others could punch with lethal force and damage their foes' internal organs. Still others could snap metal bars over their heads or poke tree bark with iron-like fingers.

"There is my house." The midwife's statement interrupted her thoughts.

Lian thanked the midwife for her help and wished her a good night.

"You think about it," the midwife said.

Lian nodded.

On her trek back, she tried to imagine how Li would fare with the monks. She would struggle to make it through a day of their brutally rigorous training.

Arriving back at her house, she found the place quiet. Only the crickets were chirping outside. On the dining table, she placed her lantern. Its dim yellow light cast shadows of their furniture and made them dance along the walls. She pulled aside the curtain to her children's room, and the light from the lantern dimly suffused it. Mei was fast asleep, a troubled expression on her face.

Beside her, Li was also asleep, tucked under her blanket. *How can I let you go?* Lian wondered.

Then she stepped over to her own bed, where she found Hai still asleep. His brows were knitted in a frown, and sweat dotted his forehead. Guarding the secret was too much pressure for him. And as Li grew, so would the pressure. Sooner or later, the villagers would find out, with catastrophic consequences.

Li's gender, this inconvenient truth, was like a boulder suspended over their heads by a pulley system. And every year they pushed it away, the higher and higher over their heads they pulled it. They might *feel* safer with the rock further away, but she knew this safety was an illusion. For a rock that falls from a greater height is even more dangerous. The rope suspending this heavy rock would eventually fray and break. And when the truth came crashing down, it would crush them.

She lowered her head to the pillow, but sleep would not come. Her thoughts, like barking dogs, kept chasing it away.

CHAPTER 5

The next morning, as Lian set down her husband's wooden breakfast bowl, she shared the midwife's proposition.

Hai ruminated over it. Silence.

"But what will happen if the monks discover the truth?" he finally asked.

Another moment of silence passed between them.

"Haaaa," Hai let out as a thought occurred to him. "But if she goes there…" he cautiously posited, "not only will she be away from the villagers, but she will also grow strong. A *Shaolin warrior*…" He let the words hover in the air. "I will be the father of a *Shaolin warrior*." He grew quiet again, taking a moment to absorb this realization. Then he turned to Lian. "Can you imagine what the villagers would think?!" He laughed heartily. "I could boast to my brother and his chubby son!"

"Let's think about this further before we decide," Lian said.

"It needs no further thought!" Hai waved her off.

"This is the best decision for all of us! Why hasn't it occurred to me before?"

Lian looked at her husband with a soft smile that put a lid on the whirlpool of emotions inside—emotions that twisted, turned, and tore her apart.

That afternoon, when Li arrived home from school, Hai painted for her a glorious image of the Shaolin Temple. He spoke of centuries-old halls, mythic statues, and the chance to learn extraordinary martial arts skills. "Whaaaoow," Li let out as she heard his descriptions.

Then he said, matter-of-factly, "We have decided to send you there."

"No!" Color suddenly rushed to Li's face. "I don't want to go! I have school," she said as an excuse.

"It is already decided," Hai replied.

Li covered her ears and forcefully shook her head, as though she would hear none of it.

Mei also rushed to Li's side. "I will not leave Li's side. If she goes, I will go with her!"

"No, Mei. The Shaolin Temple does not accept girls," Lian said. "And Li, listen. Listen, at least." Li looked at her mother, keeping her ears covered. "This will be best for all of us. There, you will become strong, and you will make our family strong—"

"You will lift our heads," Hai interjected. "The whole village will look up to us!"

As they spoke, Li's clasp around her ears got softer and softer. Then Hai took both her hands from her ears and faced her. "Please, Li. This is very important to us."

At that moment, Li felt she had no choice. She looked into her father's dark, exhausted eyes. Her shoulders, hunched from tension, lowered a little. She did love him. And though she did not understand everything he did, she understood enough that she did not want to add to his suffering.

CHAPTER 6

A few months later, once the school year was over, the day of Li's departure for the Shaolin Temple arrived. None of them had slept the previous night. They ate breakfast together in silence. Lian put Li's bag on her back and gave her a hug. In her mother's warm embrace, Li held back her urge to cry. She wanted time to stop so she could stay in that moment forever.

But then she felt someone tug at the back of her shirt. It was Mei, standing behind her, demanding a hug. She squeezed Li and kept saying, "We will visit you." She tried her best to put on a brave, smiling face, but terrible actor that she was, her face was covered with tears. Hai stood by the door, hand outstretched, and Li went to take it. They headed out together.

The sky was a dark blue, as the sun had not yet risen. Only the shapes of a few trees and hillocks were visible here and there. They walked in silence.

With every step, Li was burning with such bitter rage against her father. And the further they got from her home, the more her rage blazed. *Why did she have to be sent away? Why did her father have to separate her from her family?* But then other thoughts came, like foam, extinguishing the blaze in her heart. *He has no other choice. The other villagers forced him into this situation. And he truly loves me.* Like the tides, she went back and forth, between thoughts that arraigned and exculpated her father, and thoughts that set her heart ablaze and then washed it ashore.

The first rays of morning now glimmered from the hills, gilding the treetops and mountain peaks. Hai turned and noticed Li's drooping head. "Look," he pointed. "In the west, you can see the faint moon and the stars. Then in the east, you can see the rising sun. It's day and night, on our left and right!"

But rather than looking upwards to the heavens, Li gazed back at the path behind her and the home she was leaving behind.

Guilt coursed through Hai. *Was this the best solution?* He looked at Li's small, shaved head. Maybe they could let Li stay with them for a few more years… But scenes of the villagers discovering his lie, laughing at him, mocking him, barged into his thoughts. His fear of being exposed loomed larger than anything else. *Yes, yes, it is the best solution.* And he carried onward.

He noticed Li dragging her feet. Hai sighed. "Come, let me carry you."

Though Li could walk on her own, she wanted to punish her father. To be a heavy weight on his shoulders, just as he always put a heavy weight on hers. She hopped on his back and rested her head on the nape of his neck. Feeling his support gave her a sudden sense of serenity. Perhaps she only wanted to be closer to him, not to punish him. Wanted to affirm to herself that he loved her. She felt his body warmth. It wrapped around her like a blanket, and soon, she fell asleep.

Meanwhile, Hai could feel her slow breathing on his neck. Though he was exhausted from walking with Li on his back, he did not wish for the journey to end. For the first time, he felt a close bond with his child.

Hai took a final step forward when he saw it: the gabled roof of the Shaolin Temple.

"Li, wake up," he whispered. "We're here."

As he put her down, Li rubbed her eyes and looked above her at the grand structure.

Hai knew that the most difficult part of his journey was yet to come: convincing a Shaolin master to take Li as his student.

CHAPTER 7

Straightening his spine, Hai took a deep breath and approached the red metal gates. He grabbed the doorknocker, a golden ring in a dragon's mouth, and knocked.

Clang, clang.

A few seconds passed. There was no answer.

Clang, clang, he knocked again.

The door remained closed. As he reached to knock a third time, the heavy door creaked open, and the face of a young monk emerged. He had a shaved head and smooth, olive-complexioned skin.

"How can I help you?" he spoke gently.

"I uhh... I am looking for the shifu," Hai rasped nervously.

The monk nodded. "Follow me." He opened the door more widely, and Hai could now see the monk's saffron robes and lithe body.

They followed him to the courtyard. There stood a man dressed in earth-colored robes. He was watching the approaching figures, hands behind his back. As Hai saw him, his heart began to pound. Drawing closer, Hai could not help but be mesmerized by the man's serene and radiant aura. It bespoke a kindly nature but belied his lethal skills. The man looked to be in his early thirties yet also centuries old. His agelessness threw Hai off guard. The man gazed at them with brilliant brown eyes.

"Shifu," the monk spoke. "This man wants to see you." He departed at the master's nod.

Hai looked at the master, uncertain how to deceive him. Taking a step forward, he dropped to his knees, bowing vehemently.

"Please, Shifu, *please* take my son." He squeezed his eyes shut. "He is my only son, and I wish for him to become strong and enlightened in your ways." He bowed his head to the ground multiple times. "I beg you." And he held his breath, awaiting a response.

The master remained silent.

Although Hai's head was down, he could feel the master's gaze on Li. A frightening thought occurred to him: *What if he knows?* Sweat slid visibly down the side of his face. Desperately he tried to conceal his terror.

He took some comfort in the fact that his face was hidden; at least the master could not see his cringing expression. Yet deep down, he knew that this comfort was an illusion. The master seemed to peer right through his soul. What are the consequences of lying to a Shaolin master? He shook the question from his mind.

The master began, "We cannot—"

"PLEASE!" Hai heard himself interrupt. "He is my only son!"

The master's brows rose. He took a second look at the trembling man on the ground. When he met Li's apprehensive eyes, his gaze softened.

"What is your name?"

"Li," she spoke hesitantly.

"Li, why do you want to be a Shaolin monk?"

"I want to be a warrior, and make my father proud."

The master paused. "Is that all?

Li was unsure what to say. Confused, she added, "And I want to make my mother and sister proud?"

The master nodded, more to himself.

"The monks here train very intensely," he told her. "Are you willing to train as hard?"

This question brought fear to Li's heart. She was reluctant to commit herself to this harsh lifestyle. She gazed at her father – his eyes tightly closed, sweat dotting his forehead. This meant a great deal to him.

Li tightened her fist and met the master's gaze. "I can do it," she asserted.

The master then turned to Hai, who was still in a tense bow. He saw another drop of sweat slide from Hai's forehead onto the ground.

He asked Hai to rise to his feet. Slowly, Hai did.

Then he turned to Li. "Li, I accept you as my student."

Hai felt a burst of joy and leapt to his feet. "*Thank you! Thank you!*" He bowed deeply again, over and over. He felt like hugging the master but was too afraid to touch him, so he hugged Li, whispering in her ear, "Don't worry, we will visit you," and left.

As he walked away, Hai felt a flood of relief and elation.

Watching her father return to the gates, Li restrained her impulse to run after him. Her eyes followed until he disappeared into the distance. Then they brimmed with tears.

"You will be fine." The master's voice was gentle. Standing beside him, Li felt his calm, warm energy wash over her. She took a deep, convulsing breath and wiped away her tears.

"Come with me."

As she followed him, her eyes skimmed the series of red walls with gabled roofs. Beyond them, Li could see the tops of taller towers with multiple decks of jade-colored roofs, backed by forest-dense mountains. On her right, ancient trees thickly lined the cobblestone pathway.

Then they climbed up a series of stone staircases, each time to be greeted by a different temple building. Most had red-painted brick walls. The pillars supporting their roofs were colorful and adorned with flowery designs. Some of them were so beautiful and elaborate that Li gazed up at them in wonder. The roofs they supported were made of gray or jade-colored ceramic tiles. Patches of light green plants grew on some. Li could see hooting pigeons atop others.

Then, the master turned right, bringing them to a building in the eastern wing of a courtyard. He pulled aside a sliding door, and Li stopped short.

Inside were rows of monks seated at long wooden tables. Never before had Li seen so many people with shaved heads and orange robes in one room. At the front of the hall was a large cauldron filled with steaming rice. Behind it, an older monk scooped servings into the bowls of monks shuffling past in an orderly line.

"Eat your lunch," her shifu said. He guided her to a table bearing stacks of metal trays, bowls, and chopsticks. "Take your tray and bowls from here," he said as he handed them to her. Then he put her in line. "And stand here to be served the food."

Waiting in line, holding her tray, Li was rigid. She felt, from behind, her shifu's eyes on her. She straightened her spine in an attempt to appear strong, like the other monks. But she did not dare glance left or right; she kept her eyes fixed ahead. When her turn came, a monk filled her bowl with rice and sautéed vegetables and poured into her other bowl some soup.

Li smiled, as though she had successfully cleared one obstacle. She turned to the left where her shifu had stood, only to find that he was gone.

So she took a seat at the nearest table, then looked around. Though she was the only person here with a white shirt, no one glanced her way. All the monks ate in silence. The only sound filling the hall was that of chopsticks ticking on the bowls. Smiling at her from the center of the room was a small Buddha statue, sitting among candles.

The scent of steamed rice wafted in the air. Her stomach growled, telling her to turn her attention to her food.

She took a slurp from her soup. It was bland. She tried the rice. Bland too. She tried the vegetables and, thank goodness, they had some seasoning. She blended them with the rice and quickly ate everything.

When the monks arose to put away their trays and leave, Li found an older monk standing beside her. "You are Li?" he asked. She gazed up to see his suntanned skin, large cheekbones, and honest, dark-brown eyes beneath imperfect and scarred brows. She nodded.

"I am Kai. Shifu asked me to show you to your room."

She followed him down a corridor. He paused before a room on the left. As he opened the door, Li saw plain white walls surrounding two wooden bunk beds, a window, and a closet at the corner by the door.

"Yours is that lower one," he gestured to the bunks near the window. He then opened the closet door and pulled out a pile of robes. "These are your clothes." He handed them to her. "Good thing your head is already shaved."

She smiled.

"Shifu said you can rest today. Tomorrow, you'll start training." She nodded. "If you need anything, let me know."

As he departed, Li sat on her bed. She pressed down on the mattress with her palms. It was hard. She lay down. The pillow was thin. But with the walls close around her and the room to herself, she felt safe. *I could stay here all day.*

After a few minutes, though, she grew weary of her position and turned over. Another few minutes later, she got up. She would go out and explore.

Unfolding the garments, she slid on her robe. As she looked down at the bold orange fabric on her body, a burst of joy bubbled in her, and so did a sense of strength. Her shadow on the white wall then caught her eye. As it was late afternoon, the shadow stood taller than she. In it, she saw a monk with a shaved head and ruffled robes. Now she fit in, and with an excited smile, she headed out.

As she was walking through a courtyard, a variety of swooshing noises captured her attention. She followed the source and was led into an enclosed grassy area. There, dozens of monks armed with weapons, ranging from broadswords and chain whips to spears and staffs, were practicing their forms. They moved around, fighting imaginary foes from all corners.

A monk with a sword sliced through the air as he spun, kneeled, and struck before jumping into splits. Another monk performed multiple kicks as his chain whips gyrated around his leg, in front of his face, and behind his back, all the while without touching him. He moved with such incredible speed that Li felt like she was witnessing a silver storm. Then her attention turned to a monk training with a staff. He ran, planted his staff on the ground, and crouched atop it, like a monkey on a tree. Mimicking the monkey, he even cupped his ears and looked vigilantly to the left and right. He used the staff like a third leg, cartwheeling around it and balancing on it as he kicked in the air. When he dismounted and struck the ground, a cloud of dust rose.

Li's face froze into an awed smile and her eyes twinkled. She was in a magic show. But no, this was real. They were so nimble that they seemed weightless. They moved effortlessly, yet their strikes were direct and deadly. They were lithe, yet lethal. She knew because every time they whipped around their weapons, the air itself seemed to shriek in pain. Some of their movements were so fast as to be imperceptible to her eyes; all Li could catch was a flurry of hands and feet. She imagined the foe at the other end hitting the ground before knowing what had hit him.

Hours later, as the sun was setting, Li had dinner, then went to her room. This time, she saw the monks rooming with her. Among them was Kai, who appeared to be the oldest.

"You're back," he smiled when he saw Li enter. "Let me introduce you." Two other monks gathered around Li. There was Wei, an eight-year-old with a rather rotund body, round face, and soft features. Beside him was Qiang. He was ten, with sinewy arms, thick dark brows, and angular features.

They each greeted her and told her to let them know if she needed anything. Then they went to bed. It was only a matter of minutes before they fell fast asleep.

Lying in bed, Li turned to face the window. The full moon was glowing in the dark blue sky and illuminated a patch on the floor. A few wild dogs were barking. This was the same moon that her father had pointed out to her this morning. Now, that felt like ages ago. Already she was missing her family. She kept gazing at the moon until her eyelids grew heavy, and she fell asleep.

CHAPTER 8

Our only limits are those we set for ourselves. To break down and break free from those illusory limits, we must push ourselves. When we challenge the boundaries of our comfort zone, we expand it. What once seemed extraordinary becomes our new ordinary. When we push ourselves, we explore our human potential. When we push ourselves, we grow. Our breaking point is our making point.

Early in the morning, Li heard some shuffling noises. As she opened her eyes slightly, she found that the monks were already up, folding their blankets.

"Wake up, Li," Kai called as he aired his blanket. "Let's go."

Quickly Li grabbed her robes and took them to the bathroom, where she washed and dressed, then she headed out with the monks. Stepping into the courtyard, she saw strawberry skies wash the stone ground with the same hue. The trees around fluttered in the early morning breeze, and each was alive with the sound of incessantly chirping birds and cicadas.

The fresh air in her face forced her to take a deep breath. And when she saw the waves of monks in orange robes in the courtyard, descriptions of their legendary strength filled her head. She felt a tingling in her stomach. In her own orange robes, she ran to join them, feeling like one among them.

The monks began to run, in line formation, out the courtyard and towards the forest. A young monk instructor in his early twenties led the line. He had a cone-shaped head, pale skin, soft, almond eyes, and a jaw that jutted forward. Another monk instructor, of the same age but more tanned, was at the very back of the line. The shifu ran back and forth alongside the line, checking on each of his students. At a jogging pace, Li smiled to herself. *I can keep this up.* And when the shifu passed her, she lifted her chin and straightened her back, signaling how manageable this was for her. As he moved on, her gaze went to the light-blue mountains, and the purple ones from which the sun rose. With every step she heard the peeping of the cicadas, lending a rhythm to her jog.

Soon, they entered a forest. She ducked under a low tree branch. The morning mist descended on the trees, giving the forest a cool, ethereal atmosphere. From between the trunks, streaks of sunrays pierced the dew. The ground here, with its twigs and tree roots, became more uneven, and so did Li's breathing. She focused on the line of shaved heads in front of her. Keeping up with them became more difficult; she could barely keep up with the beating of her heart. She could not carry on. But wedged in the middle-to-back of the line, neither could she stop. She began to panic. She inhaled, and a stitch formed in her left side. She needed to stop; she needed oxygen. She couldn't carry on. She couldn't—

"All right, slow down," the shifu called, and all the monks slowed to a walk. The shifu looked at Li. She drank the air in large gulps, her shoulders rising and falling vehemently. There was snot in her nose.

They walked the expanse of the forest, and once they were out, the monks resumed their run. Once more, Li's heart beat sharply in her chest, and the stitch pierced her side. Her breaths cut short and shallow. As the monks continued, she worried that this run would never end. But soon, the Shaolin Temple was before them and they slowed to a jog. "We'll see you after breakfast," one of the instructors said. A smile appeared on Li's face, grateful for the break.

An hour later, the monks stretched and began calisthenics training.

The young monks lined up at one end of the courtyard. Then one at a time, they did various jumps, leg raises, kicks, and punches. The shifu stood at the side, closely observing each one perform in turn.

Li watched the monks in front of her, trying to memorize their every movement. When her turn approached, she puffed out her chest and stepped forward. She punched the air with full force, then kicked with the opposite leg with all her might. She glanced sidelong at the shifu, checking whether he was impressed. He remained silent.

The monks then repeated the same line of movements, and when Li's turn came again, she performed with the same level of effort as the first time.

"Li," a voice called from behind her.

She turned to find her shifu approaching. He adjusted the angles of her fists and feet. "First focus on the correct form. Then the power will come, with less effort." He slowly demonstrated to her the correct motion. She tried to emulate him. Numerous times, he stopped and corrected her.

Over time, Li's movements became sluggish. She could feel pearls of sweat rolling down her face and back. But as the monks got to the end of one line, the shifu would state, "Again... One more line... Again." And he demanded that their umpteenth movement be performed just as well as, if not better than, the one before.

Li let out a dramatic sigh, ready to move on to something new. As though not hearing it, the shifu had them go on for another hour.

"All right, take a break," he finally said.

After the monks took a water break, the shifu stood beside an ancient gingko tree. As though in silent knowing, the monks arranged around him. Li followed them. She noticed that the tree had several finger-deep holes.

The shifu ran his hands across them. "These holes were formed from the monks' training," he told her. "They would repeatedly poke the bark to strengthen their fingers." He demonstrated, his fingers filling the deep indents of the ancient tree. "These marks were not formed overnight,

but over decades. Now, centuries later, they are still here—
they endure."

A breeze brushed past them, sending a few golden
gingko leaves rolling across the courtyard behind them. Li
looked ahead: the tree stood as a testament to the power
of patience and perseverance. She tried to imagine the
ghosts of ancestors, training tirelessly around this very tree.

The shifu now looked intently at the young monks.
"Likewise, if you want your practice to persevere, you
must persevere with your practice." To internalize and
realize their martial arts skills, they had to repeat. "Repeat,
repeat, repeat," he stated. "It is not enough to know the
movement in your mind. You must know it also with
your body, so when you are fighting, you won't have to
think. You will only feel."

During lunchtime, Li gobbled down a dish of black
rice with vegetables grown in the monks' garden. Then
she took a midday nap, needing it after the morning's
intensity. It gave her the alertness and energy to continue
for her afternoon training.

The young instructor who had led their morning run
now led them to their training station. As Li followed her
group, she passed by older monks exercising on instruments
they had built themselves.

One monk hung upside down from a wooden bar by
his knees, performing a version and inversion of sit-ups. He
held a small cup in his hands. Hanging alongside him on
the bar was an empty bucket. Below him, on the ground,
was a water-filled bucket. The monk would lower himself

to the bucket on the ground and fill his cup with water. Then he would raise his body 180 degrees and empty his cup into the higher bucket. He would then lower back down to the bottom bucket, repeating until the lower bucket was empty and the hanging one was full. Then he would reverse the process.

Further ahead, a line of monks was slapping barrels of water with full force. At another corner, a monk was squatting in a horse stance. He held out a short stick horizontally with both hands. There was a long rope tied around the center of the stick and a heavy stone attached to the end of the rope. The monk would rotate the stick one way, winding the rope and hence lifting the heavy stone up. Once the rope was fully rolled around his stick and the stone lifted to its highest point, he would rotate the stick the other way, slowly lowering the stone. He repeated this multiple times.

As Li walked, she watched these monks gasp and grunt but still go on. She wondered what exercise awaited her. In a matter of moments, she would find out.

Her instructor led her group to a field containing numerous short wooden pillars. At the instructor's order, the monks stood atop them and did a horse stance. Li copied them, placing a foot on each pillar and squatting low until her thighs were parallel to the ground. It was uncomfortable. To her dismay, the instructor balanced a clay bowl on each monk's head. Sixty seconds passed. A cascade of sweat was pouring down her face. Her thighs were on fire. All her instructor did was place a hand on her shoulder. "Breathe." Another sixty seconds passed. Li's legs were wobbling violently, and she squeezed her eyes shut. The other monks were also sweating but stayed still, awaiting the instructor's order to stand. Li could not bear it anymore. She leaned forward to activate different muscle groups. But the bowl slipped past her head and shattered on the ground. She stood up, stretching her aching muscles. Kai glanced sidelong at her and bit his lips, before returning his focus to his stance. The instructor approached Li. "Thirty pushups," he ordered. While getting down to her palms and feet, Li felt embarrassed for being singled out. She struggled through these push-ups and barely made the last ones.

At the end of that day, after dinner, Li collapsed in bed. This time she fell asleep just as quickly as the other monks.

On the second day, Li could not get out of bed. Her whole body felt like it had been hit by a horse cart and lay shattered. The other monks, though, were up and folding their blankets again. She groaned.

"Li, get up," Kai called.

Two days in a row now, she had risen before the sun and headed out on a long trek. She yearned to turn away from the monks, from the temple, from all the training. To turn away in her bed, curl her legs against her torso, and with her hands beneath her cheeks, fall soundly asleep.

"It's no use," Kai responded. "If you don't push through the pain now, you will feel it again the next time we train this intensely, which is every day. Better go through with it now."

Li let out an agonizing groan. As she rose, every fiber in her back muscles pulsed with pain. She then used her hands to swing her knees to the edge of the bed. She got, albeit unsteadily, to her feet. Kai gave her a nod.

As they left, she limped after them. Every step sent pain jagging up her muscles. This morning, a run up the mountain awaited her. Their instructor stood at the base of a long, winding stone stairway. "Run! Run! Run!" he yelled as the monks sprinted up the stairway. Kai gave her a pat on the back and skipped to a sprint. Li stood behind as waves of young monks sprinted up the stairs before her. Suddenly, she felt like she was playing tag with them. With a jolt of energy, she chased after them. As she ran up, she found lush, dense foliage enshrouding the mountainside. Her eyes embraced the plants' vivid green. Their refreshing scent, moist from dew, lingered in the air.

As she climbed higher up the mountain, though, exhaustion began to seep into her. She was about to quit when the sight in front of her made her eyes twinkle. Qiang, the muscular, strong-appearing monk, was just a few feet ahead of her. *I am going to beat him*, she decided. Mustering every ounce of energy she had, she redoubled her efforts and took the steps two at a time. She got closer and closer to his back. Until. She passed him. Li felt a surge of satisfaction ripple through her. But she knew she had to keep going. With a pounding heart and wheezing lungs, she carried on. Qiang almost stopped in his path as he saw Li advance ahead of him. But he continued at his sustained pace until he found her again. This time, she was bending over her knees, vomiting.

"Come on, Li, you can keep going!"

"No, no." She waved him off with an exhausted hand. "That was everything I had."

"That was everything you had?" She nodded, palms on her knees. "Run until you reach the top. Then you can rest," he ordered her.

She wiped her mouth and took another step. Lightening pain shot across her shin.

"You can do it." Qiang stood behind her.

Despite the pain, she heaved another foot forward. One. Two. One. Two. She kept going.

"That's it!" Qiang said to her and continued running up, vanishing along the twisting stairs ahead. Li was on track again, jogging now. Every step was a battle in her head between the voices that urged her to stop and those that cheered her to keep going. She fought that battle until, to her surprise, she was on the final steps. Standing at the top, awaiting her, were the instructor and all the other monks. Her roommates cheered her on until she reached the top platform.

"You did it," Qiang said.

Li nodded, her sweaty palms on her knees as she gasped for air.

"You thought you were depleted, but you had more in you. And when you reached inside, you got that much more."

Li straightened her back. As she absorbed Qiang's words, she felt a fire ignite in her. Standing right there, atop that mountain, she felt extraordinary. In her view were the peaks of all the other dark-green mountains. The wind brushed past her sweat-covered face and cooled her wet clothes. The sun, too, was slowly rising, its golden rays dancing on the horizon. A feeling of jubilance fluttered within her heart. *I can do anything* was the motto of her moment.

"All right, now you must crab walk your way back down." The instructor's voice returned her to earth. "This exercise is meant to build muscle and strengthen the core," the instructor explained to the group.

The monks got on all fours and began crawling down the steep steps. Li gazed down, and fear crept up her spine. *What if she missed a step and fell on her face?*

"Let's go! Let's go! Let's go!" the instructor behind her yelled.

She realized she was the only one still standing there; all the other monks were already crawling down the mountain. Hesitantly, she got on her palms and toes and began descending. "Keep your body steady," her instructor intoned from behind. She tightened her core to stop the involuntary shaking, and moved down. Her eyes focused on each step ahead. One step after another, she descended the stairs. Her forearms burned and her legs trembled. *I can do it*, she told herself, taking tiny breaths in and out. From the periphery of her vision, she sensed that she was catching up to another monk. She closed in to discover that it was Wei. She could see the blood suffusing his face and his arms quaking. Finally, unable to bear the burning, he got up from his crab position and simply ran down the stairs. "Hey, that's cheating!" she called. But she kept going, Qiang's words still ringing in her head. As she reached the base of the mountain, her legs broke from beneath her and she collapsed on the ground, panting. Thankfully, what followed was stretching time.

The monks raised one foot to a wall and leaned forward, their hands holding their toes. Li closed her eyes and breathed deeply, her aching muscles savoring the stretch.

"The more flexible you are, the more pain you can endure," the instructor was saying.

Li was naturally flexible. *And that's good*, she thought. *Because I'm going to be enduring a lot of pain.*

They went through many of the same exercises from yesterday. She felt excruciating aches, and at times, she felt like crying. But despite it, and through it, she carried on. That night, random phrases swirled through her mind. She remembered her shifu's words on perseverance and Qiang's words on reaching within. Then she remembered the mountain that she'd thought would be impossible for her to scale—impossible until she stood on its summit. The Shaolin Temple constantly challenged her conception of *impossible*.

CHAPTER 9

One night, Li dreamed she was walking through hills and valleys with her family. An old wooden house stood atop one of the hills. "Go on in," her father said as he opened the front door for her. He remained outside. Behind him were her mother and Mei, smiling and waving. "Go on," he repeated. As she set foot inside, the door behind her suddenly shut. She was engulfed in pitch-black darkness, unable even to see her own hands. She turned to the door behind her and pulled at the knob. It was locked. Her heart began to pound. She knocked on the door. "Open the door!" There was no response. She knocked and called again. Silence. With her heartbeat quickening, she tried again and again, until her knocks turned to pounding and her calls became cries.

"Don't leave me alone!" she cried.

Suddenly, the house began to shake.

"Don't leave me alone!"

The earth continued to quake.

"Don't

... leave me alone."

"Don't

... leave me alone."

"I would leave you alone, but it's training time," an outside voice said.

Bewildered, Li opened her eyes. She saw Wei's face. He was shaking her. "It's training time," he repeated.

She sat up. It had been just a dream. She exhaled, and the rapid beating of her heart slowed.

At that moment, on the other side of Song Mountain, Lian suddenly felt an urge to see her daughter. "We have to visit Li," she said.

Sitting at the breakfast table, Hai shook his head. "Later, later."

"You've been saying that every day! You keep saying 'later, later,' but later never comes. We promised Li that we would visit her every two months, and now it's been much longer than that." Worrisome thoughts filled her mind. She rose to her feet. "If you don't go with us, we will go on our own."

Hai looked up at his wife and realized that he could not delay the visit anymore. He sighed. "Tomorrow, we will go." Then he headed out the door.

As he walked to the field, his thoughts chased after him. He remembered his encounter with the master. "We cannot—," he had said before Hai interrupted him. "We cannot accept girls"—is that what he had been about to say? Had he discerned Li's identity even then?

Hai worried that if they visited, the master would return Li to them. And what would happen if the villagers learned of this, that Li had been expelled from the Shaolin Temple because she was a girl?

No, no, no, he shook his head. That would not happen. *These are only thoughts.*

These are only thoughts.

These thoughts tormented him the next day, after work, as he trekked to the Shaolin Temple with his wife and Mei. He tried to control the thoughts, quiet them. As the trio drew near, the afternoon sun beat down on their heads, and Hai was sweating. The closer they got, the more intensely he sweated. He was unsure whether this was the sweat of his nervousness or of heat, or both mixed together.

Soon, he was facing a side gate of the Shaolin Temple. His hesitant hand reached for the metal doorknocker. He knocked. There was no response.

"Knock again! Knock harder!" Mei urged.

"No, just wait. Be patient," he replied.

The heavy metal door creaked open, and the face of a young monk emerged.

"Can we please see Li?" Hai said in a tremulous voice.

During break time, a monk approached Li. "There are people outside the gate, requesting you," he told her. Li got up from her seat and walked towards the gate, cautiously entertaining the thought that it could be her family.

Suddenly, at the side entrance, she saw them. Her heart hopped in delight, and she ran towards them with open arms. As she hugged them, she began to cry. "I've missed you so much!"

"We've missed you so much as well, dear!" Lian kissed her.

Mei's eyes widened. "Li! You look so strong!" Hai, too, noticed her lean muscles.

"That's because we train for hours every day," Li responded. Then she grabbed her parents' hands. "Come on, let me introduce you to my shifu and friends." She pulled them in.

Hai planted his feet on the ground. His face was pale at the idea of running into her master again. "No, no, let's not interrupt him! Let's have a family picnic outside the gates. On our way here, we found a nice spot to sit," he continued as he led her away from the gates.

They walked a few meters and reached a grassy area where a willow tree stood. Lian spread a maroon picnic cloth on the grass beneath it and took out the assorted foods she had prepared. Eagerly, the family sat around Li. As Li ate, Lian warmly rubbed her back. With light in her eyes, Li looked from her father to her mother to Mei. "Why has it taken you so long to visit?"

Lian eyed Hai without saying a word.

"So, how is your shifu?" Hai asked Li.

"Shifu's calm and knows everything. He is different from our teacher at school," she said. "I have learned so much from him."

With that, Hai took a deep breath, his mind suddenly becoming lighter. He felt now he could enjoy this family gathering, and he sat back. "You know, I told everyone in the village that you're at the Shaolin Temple," he said. "That you will become a warrior! And I—"

Mei cut him off and erupted, "Li! Tell us, how is your life as a monk?"

Li swallowed her food and answered. "Every day here, I learn new skills."

As though remembering something, she suddenly gasped. "Mei! Let me teach you how to walk on your hands!"

Mei eagerly turned her full attention to her.

Li demonstrated. "Stand with your arms up to your ears… Step forward and raise one leg at a time…"

"Now," her voice was strained as she stood upside down. "Move one hand slightly forward, leaning in that direction, then the other…" She kept walking forward on her hands.

Mei clapped her hands. "Whoa!"

"Li, get down! You just ate; your food will come up!" Lian scolded.

Li obeyed, laughing. Seeing the happiness on her face, Lian smiled. She felt her daughter was in a good place.

For an hour, they sat together as she shared with them her experiences at the Shaolin Temple.

Soon, the sun began to descend, casting shadows of the trees on the valley.

"Now, we have to leave," Hai said. "We need to get back home before dark, and you need to go back to the Temple."

Li compressed her lips, unwilling to let her family go, especially not after being reminded how fun it was to spend time with them. But they promised they would visit again. The visit gave her some peace of mind and enough contentment to go through many more challenges.

CHAPTER 10

Between her intense training sessions, Li found calmness in her calligraphy class. There were rows of low-lying wooden tables and accompanying pillow seats. On each table were large, white sheets of paper, a brush, and a jar of black ink. She enjoyed making a stroke on the paper, completely absorbed in the one act.

One afternoon, Li was sitting in the middle of the class, painting her characters. Then, from the corner of her eye, she noticed a monk struggling with his brush. His hand was unsteady, leaving jagged lines and deep blotches of ink on the paper.

When she raised her gaze to his face, she froze, as though staring at a ghost. He had pale skin and big, light-blue eyes. Never had she seen someone like him before.

She whispered to the monk sitting beside her, "Do you see him? What happened to him?"

The monk brought his head near her ear. "I don't know, because he speaks very little Chinese. But he says he came from America, and that his head hurt."

"*Ahhh!*" Li made the connection. His head hurt so much that his eyes must have turned blue.

Now she took pity on the boy whose head hurt. She approached him and grasped his hand. "When you start a new character," she said, "you must press down on the brush in one continuous movement." She moved his hand slowly down the paper. "And then, when you're nearing the end, slowly lift the brush off the paper."

He turned his head to her. "Wow. Thank you for your help."

Li smiled and kept staring at his blue eyes.

She saw him again the next class, and the class after that. And through the weeks, she befriended this monk, whose name was David. Everyone called him by his Chinese name, Dawei. His funny characters and broken Mandarin made her develop an affinity for him.

In their break time, they would walk along the tree-lined paths of the Shaolin Temple. Sometimes, Li would display the English words she had learned in school. Pointing to a farmer walking his beast, she would say, "Horse!"

"That's actually a mule," he would correct her.

As he spoke mostly in English and she mostly in Mandarin, they could not discuss complex subjects. But they could teach each other the basics of their respective languages. She yearned to learn English so she could better understand and communicate with him. Occasionally, Li would ask, "When will your head get better?" or "When will your eyes turn brown again?" Not understanding, he would change the subject.

One afternoon a few months later, David's mother came for a visit. David introduced Li to her. Upon seeing the mother, Li's eyes flew wide with surprise. *His mother's condition is even worse!* she thought. *Her hair had even turned yellow!*

"Mother, this is the monk I told you about, who teaches me Mandarin," David introduced.

"Ahh, I am so pleased," the mother smiled and shook Li's hand. "Thank you Li… We have something for you," she said in English.

She reached into her leather handbag while Li stared at her golden hair. Then Li saw held out before her a rectangular object in red giftwrapping and a yellow bow.

"It's a present," David said excitedly. "You can open it."

Her lips parted in surprise and joy, Li tore the wrapping and slid out the object. It was a teach-yourself English book.

"Whoaw! Thank you!" Li's eyes glowed.

"I told my mother that you wanted to learn English. So she went and got you this. As you get better, we can get you the next levels," David said.

"Thank you so much!" Li bowed and spoke to the mother in English.

From that day on, Li spent her afternoon breaks studying English. She would then practice the sentences she learned with David. And true to his promise, as she improved, he got her more advanced English language books. While he would tell her about America, she would share with him her knowledge of Chinese culture.

One autumn afternoon, Li was passing the western wing of a courtyard when a familiar voice halted her.

"For how much longer do I take these?"

That is David, she thought. She leaned closer to the slightly ajar door and peered in.

David was speaking to the Shaolin doctor. He was a man in his early forties, dressed in light gray attire. He always smiled slightly when speaking. Three large posters of the human anatomy, showing the meridians, hung on the milky wall beside them. Against the front wall was a sink, and above it, a cabinet with some jars and boxes. Two patient beds with white sheets lay in the center, and a dark wooden chair stood by the corner of the back wall. The Shaolin doctor now handed David a few bags of herbal medicine.

She stepped back. *It has been almost a year now. Does his head still hurt?*

That night, the moon was watching over the gabled roofs of the library below, and hanging under the roof were two glowing red lanterns. Crickets' chirps sounded from within the bushes. Li and David were sitting on the library steps.

"I saw you with the Shaolin doctor today," Li began. "How is your head?"

This time, she knew enough English to speak to and sufficiently understand him.

"It is good," he said.

Li still looked at him. "What happened to your head before?"

David was quiet. He lay back on the cool stone platform, hands clasped behind his head, and gazed at the faint clouds that passed over the pale, round moon. "It was in middle school when I first felt sick and began to feel pangs of pain in my head," he said. "I learned that I had a tumor in my brain. The doctor said I had a short time left to live—" His voice broke.

Li looked at him with consternation.

"I tried every type of treatment and medication," he continued. "None of them worked. It was as though I was just waiting for death to take me."

He grew quiet. In the dark, they could hear a crumpled leaf roll across the cobblestones.

"Then one of my father's friends suggested I try traditional Chinese medicine, which views an illness as just an imbalance in the body. Given the proper lifestyle, the body could restore that balance. My father's friend recommended my parents send me to the Shaolin Temple. He said the lifestyle here cleansed people's bodies and cleared their minds."

He rose to his elbows. "My parents didn't believe in this, but I was drawn to its optimism. In Western medicine, my diagnosis was like a death sentence. In Eastern medicine, I had hope. My parents finally decided that since nothing else was working, there could be no harm in trying. And I might as well spend the last months of my life doing something I loved."

"Shifu graciously accepted me. And we worked to restore what he calls 'the yin and yang balance' in my body."

He sat up fully. "Here, I exercise together with the brother monks. I pray and meditate. I eat food from our vegetable garden and drink herbal medicine. I spend hours in nature. And every day, rather than think of myself as slowly dying, I am focused on living."

He glanced sidelong at Li. "I don't know if I was mis-diagnosed, or if my tumor has truly shrunk. But I know this: more than a year has passed, and I have never felt more alive." There was a sparkle in his blue eyes.

"So when will your eyes turn brown again?" Li asked. "Since your head doesn't hurt anymore."

David looked at her, at first confused. Then he broke into laughter. "That will never happen. I was born with blue eyes."

She laughed at herself now.

The trees seemed to shake off the day in the evening breeze.

CHAPTER 11

Days continued turning to weeks, and weeks to months, and years later, Li stood much taller and stronger. Her facial features had grown sharper. Her muscles were more toned and her bones denser. With her years of training, she now had the agility, strength, and stamina to specialize and take her skills to greater levels.

She was standing in the courtyard, eyeing her sparring opponent; other monks were sitting, spectating. Li took cautious steps, circling around him. He was a big, stocky monk named Bao, and he moved with strength and directness. She continued to circle.

Suddenly, she threw a kick to his head. As he blocked it with his arms, she did a spin kick to his now unguarded stomach.

"*Ooff!*" Bao let out. He receded a few steps.

She bounced around now, feeling like she owned the ring. Sparring was more than a fight to her. It was a game of chess. It was strategically setting up her opponent for his downfall. She avoided looking directly at where in her opponent's body she planned to target, so as not to telegraph her intentions. She'd stared intently at his sternum, bringing his attention to that area, only to punch him in his face. If her opponent had a tendency to move in a particular rhythm—*one-two-one-two*—she took notice, then broke his rhythm by striking in the one-and-a-half beat, throwing him off guard. She changed up her own pace to be unpredictable.

And she changed up her style. There was a saying that the best style was no style. Every opponent had a unique physique—a different reach, height, speed, movement pattern, and more. She knew that the same strategy that worked for one person may not for another. She couldn't always rely on using the linear, aggressive style of a big person, as there would always be someone bigger than she was. She could not rely solely on her speed, as there would always be someone quicker. She had to size up and slow down, forcing herself to adapt to and adopt different approaches.

If the sparring platform was the chessboard, then she was the queen—adopting the styles of different pieces on the board but not having a style of her own. Perhaps that was her style.

She did a final leg sweep, sending Bao to the ground. Her roommates cheered. A cool burst of air brushed the sweat on the back of her neck and, standing straight, she smiled.

Her toughest battle, however, was an internal one. As she had reached adolescence, Lian had advised her on how to guard her identity as a man while taking care of herself as a woman. Every time her mother gave her tips, Li's gaze would drop to the ground and her cheeks would burn. But beneath her embarrassment was a growing rage.

She despised having to be an imposter around her friends, and on guard while they were all relaxed. Whenever her mother lowered her voice, sharing information as though it were a secret just between the two of them, she yearned to snap at her and scream.

She despised being born a girl. When she saw herself in the mirror, she scrunched up her face, her fists wanting to shatter her reflection to pieces. Every day, she wrapped cloth around her chest tighter and tighter, as though the fabric could one day flatten her chest completely.

She channeled her rage into her training. If the monks rose before the sun, then she rose before them, and she trained longer into the night. She went through her forms and stances over and over again. She stared at the gingko trees with their multiple holes, and at the ancient depressions on the ground of the training hall. In them she would jab her fingers or pound her feet repeatedly, following the movements of imagined ancestors. She wanted to hit herself hard, hard, hard until she hardened. She felt a gigantic anger within, yearning to rip apart this corpse of her body and let her giant spirit out. She wanted to roar and let the mountains echo, to soar and let the clouds be her bedding.

But she could not release her vortex of rage. She could not tell her shifu or the other monks without exposing her secret. Nor could she vent to her family. Whenever she looked into her father's cowardly eyes, she saw a man too feeble to stand against the tides of tradition. Screaming at him would only make him suffer more, without changing her state. So she carried on as an obedient daughter. But beneath her surface performance, she was crumbling inside. Within her emotions, she was buried alive.

She knew, though, that her rage was only burning herself. She remembered her shifu's teaching: when the world outside feels beyond your control, tune in to the world inside. She would turn, as her shifu taught her, to meditation as her outlet. Sitting by a tree at the base of the mountain, she would close her eyes and focus on her breath, in and out. In and out. She felt the air rush in through her nose and expand her belly. She inhaled the fresh air and calmness into her body. She exhaled all her toxic rage and worry. As she repeated, slowly her muscles let go of their tension, and she let go of her thoughts. She let them drift by without any judgment or attachment. She saw them drift by as if she were a side observer, watching the wind carry leaves. Soon her senses sharpened to the present moment. She could hear the symphony of nature, the trees whispering to one another.

How giving nature is. She listened to the singing of the birds and thanked them for their music. She savored the fragrance of the flowers and thanked them for their perfume. Lying under the canopy of a tree, she thanked it for its shelter. Seated on the grass, she thanked it for its carpet. She thanked the sun for its light and the sky for its canvas of color. She was a part of nature, and nature was a part of her. Everything was whole, and she was in harmony.

When she got up from a meditation session, she felt much lighter. She walked the earth with a nimble grace, kissed the floor with her feet, embraced the air with her lungs, and hugged the world with open arms. She was living in the present moment, and this moment was a present.

CHAPTER 12

One afternoon, Hai was tilling the earth. A few rooks stirred from a nearby tree and, one after another, flew over the sunbaked fields. There was the sound of the chatter of an approaching group of men. Resting his hoe on the ground, Hai placed a hand to his forehead and squinted. He saw his brother Feng, accompanied by three men in business suits, surveying the land. To Hai's dismay, Feng gestured over to the area where Hai was working. He dropped his hoe and ran over to them.

"Hey Feng, what's going on?"

Feng turned his back to Hai and, walking forward, kept talking to the men. "Yes, this land has very rich soil."

Hai paused. *Why is he telling them about the land?* He followed them.

"What's going on? Who are these people?"

Feng quickened his pace, leading the men away from Hai. "Shall I show you the rest of the land?"

Seeing they were ignoring him, Hai stayed behind, staring at them until they were four dots in the distance.

A fellow farmer approached him. "Hai, have you heard?" Hai turned to the farmer behind him, attentive. "Your brother wants to sell this land's rights to a big agricultural company."

Hai's mouth dropped. "*What?!*"

"He will use the money to open a supermarket in the city," the farmer continued.

No, this can't be, Hai thought. He depended on this land to feed his family.

Although the farmer was still standing beside him, Hai no longer noticed. Without saying another word, he headed home. When he opened the front door, Lian remarked, "You're back early today." Then she noticed his pale face.

"What happened?!" She rushed to his side and, holding his hand, led him to a chair.

He sat slowly and spoke as though in disbelief. "My brother wants to sell our land rights to a big agricultural company." His voice was laced with despair, as though he had already given up and just wanted his wife to comfort him.

Lian took a moment to absorb this. Then she spoke. "Why don't you go talk to your brother. Ask him to give you your rightful share of the money, or at least to leave us a parcel of land to live off. After all, this was *your* land."

Hai tensed at the suggestion of standing up against his brother. His brother's word was law, even when Feng was robbing him. His wants took priority, even over Hai's needs. His acts were justified, even if they were not just, because he was the powerful one. And he was the older one—the one whom the village feared and revered.

A gentle hand on his forearm brought his attention back. "Talk to him tomorrow," Lian said softly.

Hai looked up into his wife's eyes. Shame suddenly crept into him. *How could he let his own family down? How could he tell his wife that he couldn't provide for them, just because he was too afraid to challenge his brother?*

"I will talk to him tomorrow," he said.

Lian nodded, but his words did not bring her relief. She knew his brother was malicious, and she did not want to be at the mercy of such a man.

The next day, instead of heading to the fields, Hai went to his brother's new house for the first time.

For every step forward, he yearned to take two steps back. Too soon, he was facing Feng's maroon main gates. He took a deep breath. He was going to do it. He was going to walk in there and ask his brother to give him his due. He raised his hand and gave the door a knock.

A few seconds later, a servant opened the door. Hai told him he was here to see his brother, so the servant led him to the courtyard.

Hai gazed around at his brother's massive courtyard. Organized around its sides and front were the living quarters, with slanted black tile roofs. His gaze skimmed the grape vines that clawed along the walls. A bush of Chinese roses, deep blood red, grew in one corner, and some potted plants stood in other corners. At the center was a stone fountain, and a flash of gold caught Hai's eye. As he peered in, he saw the backs of swimming koi. He continued onward.

"Hello, hello," a high-pitched voice called, startling him.

As he turned, he saw a large, rectangular cage filled with a motley mixture of colorful parrots and other birds.

"Hello, hello."

Hai now looked at the green parrot calling him. Its claws gripped the metal screen of the cage, and its head moved left and right, observing Hai.

What a life his brother was living! He was awash in riches yet would leave Hai to live in a mud shack. His fists tightened.

"Hello, hello. Sir?" This time it was the servant. "This way, please." Hai shook off his reverie and followed.

The servant opened a door and led him into a scarlet living room. Hai stopped in his tracks. Around forty villagers were sitting and chattering on red velvet sofas that lined either side of the living room. Hai quickly seated himself in a vacant space on the sofa nearest to the door.

On the wall in front of him was a large painting of two golden fish. As he gazed at it, the sound of everyone talking swirled around the room.

Hai leaned toward the other villagers on his sofa. "Why is everyone here?" he whispered.

"Your brother is opening a grand supermarket in the city," the villager beside him said.

"So we came to ask him to give us jobs there," a second added.

Suddenly, a villager scurried into the hall. "He's coming! He's coming!" As everyone hushed, they heard footsteps approaching. Then Feng appeared. All the villagers rose to their feet.

Feng walked to the center of the room. "What can I do for you?"

"We would like jobs in your new supermarket," a villager shouted.

"My son just finished school, and he is good at counting," another said. "Can he work as a cashier?"

Feng made a show of pondering for a while. Then he spoke. "When I fully establish my new supermarket, I will be happy to employ you."

This ignited a roar. Cheers broke out, and the villagers applauded. Feng's eyes next fell on his younger brother. Hai felt encouraged by his brother's generous mood. Hesitantly, he approached the center of the room. The time this took seemed extraordinarily long.

"I am happy for your success, my brother," he said, fiddling with his fingers. "I was wondering, if it was okay, if I, ah—" Hai's tongue felt heavy, unable to carry his words. His sentence fell apart. He had to muster his courage to finish his request. "If I could have my share of money from the land, or keep a small piece of my land, so my family could live off of it…"

Crimson suffused Feng's neck, ears, and face. "*What?! What did you say?*" he yelled. "*Your land? This is my land, mine alone!*"

All the villagers fell silent and turned their heads to the drama unfolding at the center.

"But, but... we are of one blood. I have some rights to this land as well," Hai stammered.

"Let me clear this up for you." Feng let out a cold laugh that froze Hai's blood. Feng paced around the room, looking at the villagers' solemn, reverent faces, savoring the moment. "Take one cup, and pour water in it. Then put a few drops of oil in it. What will happen?"

The villagers stirred, unsure where he was going.

"What will happen?!" he bellowed.

Hai froze.

"I will tell you..." Feng growled in his ear. "The oil will rise to the top, no matter what. No matter how much water is below. No matter that the two substances are in the same cup. The oil will always rise to the top! Because they are made of different things."

Gasps escaped from some of the villagers.

"This land is mine," he continued. "I've already given you more than you deserve."

Hai felt the eyes of the villagers hot on his face and immediately wished he were elsewhere. But mercilessly, his brother continued.

"Instead of having your son slap the water, or kick the air, or chop the wood," he made a show of motions mimicking these actions, "let him come here and help you!"

The whole room erupted into laughter. All the villagers had at one point or another over the years been subjected to Hai's boasts about his warrior son and the family land. But now, in a matter of seconds, Feng had made a mockery of his nephew's monkhood and revealed that the leased "family land" was actually Feng's alone.

Everywhere he looked, Hai saw glittering eyes, red, guffawing faces, and pointing fingers. *No, no, no, this couldn't be happening.* His mind scrambled desperately to make sense of the situation. It was a nightmare. *This isn't really happening,* he repeated to himself, his pulse and breathing accelerating. He turned and turned, as though turning in bed. But no matter where he turned, he still found himself at the center of a jeering crowd. He felt like prey, his reputation pounced upon from all directions and shredded to pieces. He had dedicated his whole life to building a respectable reputation among these villagers. Now, his brother had destroyed it in seconds. His mouth and eyes froze open in horror.

Feng looked before him and saw a broken man. With the villagers behind him, he puffed out his chest and sneered down on his brother. "Show me! What are you going to do now? Huh?" Feng lifted his chin. The villagers continued snickering.

It was all Hai could do to gather the broken pieces of his self-respect and raise a single, wagging finger. "You will see! You will see! One day, you will see!" Having nothing in the present, he threw everything upon the future.

This incited even further laughter and jeering. Against this background din, unable to utter another syllable, Hai sought to run away. But his feet felt so heavy they refused to comply. As he turned to the exit and placed a foot forward, he tripped and sprawled facedown. The villagers let out another uproar of laughter. Hai quickly picked himself up, then squirmed his way through the villagers and out the door.

As he staggered back home, his heart was still racing. He kept his eyes fixed to the ground, unable to meet anyone's gaze. He wished the earth would swallow him whole. Not only had he become the laughingstock of the village. But now, he had to face his family. Tell them he could not provide for them. He wished that he did not have to go home. But neither could he bear to stay out in the village, risking a run-in with the villagers.

His mud house was now before him. His hands fumbled around the doorknob, and as soon as he opened the door, he dove straight under his bed covers.

Lian needed no further explanation. She sat beside him while he shook beneath the blankets. To confirm her surmise, though, she slowly asked, "What happened?"

At the question, Hai's mind replayed the scene from his brother's house. Silent whimpers escaped him, quickly becoming weeping and then wailing. Lian grew quiet. The agony in his cries already conveyed to her the unutterable story.

From the adjacent room, Mei heard her father's misery. It was the first time she had heard him cry. The sound drew tears to her eyes and left bitterness in her heart.

CHAPTER 13

For days, Hai did not set foot outside the house. The walls felt like a shield from the eyes of the villagers. One afternoon, Mei came home from the village market. She was carrying a platter of vegetables over her head. With great haste, she placed it on the dinner table and entered her parents' room. Her father was sitting in bed, drinking green tea, and her mother was at his side.

"Everyone in the market was saying, talking, it was—" she fumbled over her words, then restarted. "I heard today that Uncle officially sold the land rights for a huge profit. Everyone in the market was talking about it."

Hai's hands fidgeted. Lian took the teacup from him. It was official: he could no longer use the land.

"Our land had the richest soil," Hai mumbled. "For a long time, this land was our pride. All the villagers thought—"

"Father, *please*," Mei snapped, "for one moment, stop caring so much about what others think of us and start caring about your family." Hai was stunned into silence.

Seeing an opening, Mei continued with greater zeal. "You worry so much about the people who don't like you that you forget those who *love* you. You live your whole life according to what they think is right rather than what is right for you." She felt anger course through her veins, tightening her fists. "You do nothing that challenges their expectations. You say nothing that opposes their views. And now, you wonder why you're nothing."

Pain flickered in his eyes, and she knew she had gone too far. But she could not stop now. All those years, she had watched him bow to people's opinions, and she hadn't said a word. But this—seeing him, right there, cowering under his covers rather than taking care of them—was his lowest point yet. Everything she had ever yearned to tell him over the years escaped from her at that moment.

"You let their ideas of how one should live dictate *our* lives too," she continued, still standing in the doorway. "You made Li deny her very nature just so you could concede to society's expectations. You—"

"Mei! Enough!" Lian yelled, but Hai raised his hand as though to say, *Let her continue.*

Mei did go on. "You act like this land's rights were yours, even though you knew your brother seized it from you. If all those years, you had spent your energy elsewhere, we would've had much more than we do now. Instead of challenging your fears, you feed them. You say your brother is the enemy. But really, you're your own biggest enemy. If I were you," she pointed forcefully from her to him, "I would get out from under that blanket, get out of the house, and look for other work." The bitterness in her tone surprised even herself.

"We don't need your wisdom, Mei!" Lian rose to her feet, having heard enough. "You're twenty-two years old now; if you were so smart, you would have found a husband for yourself!"

Sensing a fiery fight arising, Hai suddenly pulled the blanket over his head and turned over. This sent Mei and Lian quietly, though bitterly, out of the room to let him rest.

After darkness had fallen, while his family was asleep, Hai got up and stole out of the house. The glowing moon above met him and illuminated the valley. A gentle breeze brushed his nose, carrying with it the scent of the earth. He strolled past the fields and along the village's empty pathways. The village was asleep, and he could see their small, weather-worn houses, some with clothes left hanging outside, the night air blowing through them. A sense of serenity overcame him. He didn't have to please anyone here, as there was no one awake to please. For the first time, he saw the village with different eyes. And he saw the villagers for what they were: simply people trying to live their own lives. *Why did I make a big deal out of them?* he wondered. Perhaps if he had seen them this way much earlier, he would have focused on his own life as well, and lived more peacefully with himself and his family.

Leaving the village behind, he neared his former cornfields. Droplets of water sat on the leaves, sparkling like diamonds under the moon. He looked up. Even though he was under a canopy of stars, he could only see the darkness between.

He thought of what Mei had said. Every word was true, he knew. But now, he was too tired. He had expended too much of his life trying to please others; he had no energy left to change himself. It was too late for him. As his eyes fell on the path in the distance, leading to the Shaolin Temple, he remembered Li. A pang of guilt hit him. She was always trying her best to make him proud. But what had he ever done to raise her head? He felt guilty for forcing her to live against her nature. He felt guilty for separating her from her family. He felt guilty for making his family live under challenging conditions. He felt guilty for deceiving himself, for wasting his life.

He trudged back home with a heavy heart. In front of him was his small, mud house, its walls chipped and cracked. The only thing big in this house, he acknowledged, was his ego. As he pushed past the creaking door, he found Mei asleep. Distress marked her face. *I'm sorry for what I did to you, Mei... No,* he corrected, *I'm sorry for what I didn't do for you.* He walked over to his wife. She was mumbling something in her sleep. *I'm sorry for making your life more difficult.* As he dropped to his bed, a tear slid down his cheek and onto his pillow. He pulled the blanket over his head.

CHAPTER 14

The next morning, the sun washed into the room, revealing dust particles hovering in the air.

Lian gently shook Hai to wake him up. "Hai, it's almost noon."

He didn't respond.

She shook him again, harder this time. "Hai, wake up."

Still there was no response.

As she swept away his blanket, the hairs on the back of her neck rose. She found a body with no soul.

"*Mei!*" she screamed.

Mei rushed into the room and found her mother pale, stuttering words she could barely pronounce. "Your ... your f-father's not answering. Ca-call the doctor! Ru-run!"

"*What?!*" Mei looked at her father, eyes wide with fear.

"*Go!*" Lian shouted.

In a great panic, Mei scrambled out of the house and to the village. She was soon back with the village's new doctor in tow. The doctor checked the body, feeling for a pulse at Hai's wrist.

Mei was biting her nails, and her mother was clasping her hands, nails digging into her skin.

Gently, the doctor lowered Hai's wrist, then drew the blanket over his head.

As he turned to the family, his eyes were somber. "I'm sorry. He passed away, probably from a heart attack."

"No," Mei breathed. "No! No! No!" She dropped onto her father's chest and shook her head. "I'm sorry, Father. I'm sorry. This is all my fault. I didn't mean to—" her voice croaked. As she squeezed her eyes shut, her tears wet his blanket.

The doctor quietly saw himself out of the house.

Mei inhaled against the blanket, and when she spoke again, her voice was hoarse.

"Father, I love you." She shook him. "Father, do you hear me? *I love you*," she kept repeating, wishing these had been the last words he had heard, not her angry rant from yesterday.

Lian stood paralyzed as the world spun beneath her at a dizzying speed. This was a nightmare. But seeing her daughter mourn at her husband's bedside made the somber reality seep in. Her knees felt weak. She collapsed on a chair, weeping.

The only sounds in the house were the two women's sobs. They cried and cried until their eyes were dry and swollen.

Lian finally took in a deep, trembling breath. She turned to Mei. "We are on our own now."

Mei removed her head from her father's bed and stared at her with hollow eyes. "Mother, please tell me, is this real? Is this really happening?"

She kept staring at her mother, waiting.

"Mei, we need to think of how we are going to survive. I need you to get Li."

Mei slowly rose from her father's bedside and, eyes still stinging, left the room.

She opened the house door and thought, *All our problems came from outside this door.* She slammed it.

As she walked, her feet pounded on the ground, as though yearning to beat the earth.

A few farmers were in the green fields. As she passed them, they looked up and called. "Mei! Mei!"

She clenched her jaw and kept walking.

"Hey Mei!" another called.

She walked faster now. More forcefully.

"How is your father doing? We haven't seen him for a couple of days."

Tightening her fists, she almost broke into a run.

"Where is your father?"

Suddenly, she stopped and spun around, color rushing to her face. "MY FATHER IS DEAD! HE IS DEAD!" she screamed. Bringing her forearm to her face, she wiped her watery eyes and erupted into a sprint.

She hated everything. Hated her uncle. Hated these farmers. Hated the earth. Hated the trees that fluttered obliviously in the breeze. Mostly, she hated herself.

She could run from everything around her, but she could not run from the guilt churning within.

He was already suffering. And I put more pressure on him. Her mother had warned her to hush up, she'd warned her. But she and her big mouth had just carried on. She bit her lips.

As she ran, memories of yesterday's insolence were running through her mind, tears were running down her face, and boiling blood was running through her veins. Her father's time had run its course. *Run, run, run! You idiot! Run until you run out! Run until you wither away!*

A tree root caught her foot, and she tripped forward, landing hard. Her palm and forearm were scraped and bloodied. Dirt clung to her face and body, as though the earth sought to take its revenge on her. She rose, flicking the dirt from her forearms and clothes. Then she looked at the culprit. Forcefully, she kicked the tree root. "*Stupid thing!*" she yelled. "All our life is stupid obstacles." She kicked it again.

As she turned away, she began walking more slowly. Pain coursed through her body.

"We are on our own now," her mother had said. The tremor in her mother's voice frightened Mei. *What will we do?* She had no answer. The mix of emotions within her, along with the tiring trek, clouded her mind.

Finally, she was met with the gabled roofs of the Shaolin Temple.

It was late afternoon, and Li was training with her weapons in the courtyard. A monk approached. "Someone at the gate is here to see you."

She dropped her staff and walked over. She was not expecting any visitors. *Who could it be?*

For the first time, seeing her sister by the gates did not please her. Mei's face was stained with tears and dirt. "Mei, what's wrong?" Li ran over to her.

"Li, Father's dead!" Mei wailed.

Li froze. She could not believe the words that had just washed into her ears. "*What?* How? When?" she sputtered. "But—but I just saw him last month. He was fine."

Mei shook her head. "The doctor thinks he had a heart attack."

Li could only gaze blankly when Mei said, "We have to go home, before it gets dark. I'll tell you more on the way."

On their trek home, Mei told Li about their father's visit to their uncle's house, and her own rant from yesterday. The sun's head was sinking below the purple mountains. Wild dogs began to howl. Li and Mei walked silently now, each absorbed in her own thoughts.

At nightfall, everything around them was dark, and there was only the sound of their footsteps on dirt.

From the distance came the light of a lantern or two. As the farmers carrying them neared, the light glowed on Li's and Mei's somber faces. "Sorry for your loss. He was a good man," they expressed.

Li nodded mutely, but Mei brushed past them with bitter disregard. At last, they were facing their own mud house. As Li creaked open the door, she heard the sound of their mother weeping. Entering her parents' dimly lit room, she found a blanket-covered body on the bed and her mother beside it.

Lian rose and drew the blanket back from Hai's face so Li could see her father one last time. Li stepped forward.

As she beheld him, tears formed in her eyes. She bit her lips, trying to hold back the sobs that had threatened during the entire return journey.

He was only in his early forties, yet so many more years had seemed to weigh on him. His eyes were closed, and his face no longer had lines of worry or fear. *Finally,* she thought, *he is at peace.*

CHAPTER 15

The prayer ceremony began on a morning a few days later. Hai had always wished to be buried in his land. But since the land was no longer his, and they could not afford a burial site, they decided to have him cremated.

Many of the villagers, Hai's fellow farmers and neighbors, were gathered in the open field. In somber colors, they stood—the sad, the indifferent, and the indifferent who pretended to be sad.

Hai's family was dressed in black. Li watched while, in the center of the field, flames consumed her father's body. As she saw the smoke rise, she thought of the family land, her father's aspirations for wealth and worldly status. All the things he had been attached to throughout his life he could not truly take with him in the next. *What a fleeting thing life is,* she thought. *The only thing we take with us is our memories, and the only thing we leave behind is our legacy.* She thought of the memories that could enrich a life. *Did we cherish moments with our families? Did we stay up all night with the stars, or see sunrise paint the sky? Were we present in our lives, or were we living in our heads?* Sparks were hovering in the smoke. A breeze stirred, brushing against her face and sending the smoke sideways. She thought of what made a legacy meaningful. *Were we proud to be us? Did we have the courage to live the life we wanted? Did we let go of our fears? Or did we hold on to our grudges? Did we develop ourselves every day, or were we slowly dying? Did we give like we were the richest persons in the world, or were we always afraid of being poor?*

While Li was absorbed in her thoughts, Mei, from the corner of her eyes, glanced at their uncle Feng and his son behind him. Feng was staring at the ground with a somber expression. His son, chubby and in his mid-twenties, also had his head down.

As she sensed them now approaching, Mei elbowed Li, rousing her from her thoughts.

"I am so sorry about your loss," said Feng as he handed Lian a bouquet of white irises. The son behind him nodded, not meeting their eyes.

Lian accepted the flowers without revealing any emotion. "Thank you for coming."

Feng frowned, scratched his head. "I did not expect him to leave us so early. But what can we do? That is what was written for him."

Lian kept quiet.

He looked at Mei, about to say something to her, but saw that she remained staring at the ground, frowning. So Feng turned to Li, the more even-tempered of the two. "I am sorry for your loss." He shook her hand. Li looked at him. Although it had been years since she had last seen her uncle, time's passing did not show on his face. "If there is anything I can do for your family," he said, "let me know."

This was unexpected for Li. She kept her gaze on him but remained silent.

"Ah..." He stood there awkwardly. Seeing nothing more for him to do, he took his leave. His son followed after him.

Li looked behind at them as they walked away. *Could his brother's death have changed him?* she wondered.

For weeks, Li ruminated over her uncle's offer of help. She had sensed some remorse in his voice. Perhaps he felt guilty about their father and was now more willing to help. She shared with her mother her plan to talk to him: she would ask for their lawful share from the sale of the land rights.

Lian shook her head. "No, no, no. I know this man. He could never change. Don't let his nice words deceive you."

"If he truly felt guilty," Mei jumped in on the conversation, "he would not have arranged for his son's wedding to happen so soon after the funeral."

"We have to give him a chance," Li insisted. "I will talk to him."

The next afternoon, Li visited her uncle's house. It was packed with villagers preparing for his son's wedding.

Some were hanging decorations and lights along the gabled roofs squaring the courtyard. Others swept the ground and set up tables of food. The aroma of delicious cooking, the sounds of music, and the din of conversation all mixed in the air.

As Li stepped into the courtyard, all heads turned towards the monk in orange robes. They looked on at her with amusement.

"I heard his mother and sister are now working as housemaids," a woman whispered to those around her.

"Coming back from the Temple?" a villager sneered.

"Go find a real job to support your family," another villager yelled.

"I know what job is good for you..." a man said with great alacrity.

"Chopping wood!" another added. And he imitated the motion of chopping woods with his hands.

They all laughed. Li maintained her focus on her uncle.

Feng was seated on a wooden chair outside, a plate of cake and biscuits on his lap, and giving orders to two villagers hanging lights on the roof. From the corner of his eye, he saw Li approaching. *What is he doing here?* He gritted his teeth.

The closer Li got to him, the more intense the villagers' whispers became. As Li finally stood before her uncle, all the whispering ceased. Everyone was attentive.

"Li!" Feng rose from his seat. "I did not expect you here, so soon after your father's funeral. Nonetheless, it is a pleasure to see you."

"Thank you, Uncle, and congratulations to my cousin on his marriage."

"Hopefully your wedding will come soon too. Oh!" His eyes widened, and his hand covered his mouth. "Forgive me, I forgot; you're a Shaolin *monk*! You will *never* get married!"

The villagers broke into another round of laughter.

Li kept her gaze on her uncle. "At the funeral, you said if we needed anything, we should let you know. I would like to take you up on your offer." He raised his eyebrows. "I am here to talk about our family land," she continued.

The sound of the words "our family land" irked him. Regaining some of his composure, Feng pretended to fume. "First your father, then you. How many times do I have to explain this? Wait, wait—" He raised his hands, as though to gather the attention of all the villagers in the courtyard. They duly looked at him.

"You, you, and you!" He pointed to some villagers standing around. "I remember you were all witness to what I told his father. Tell him." Feng turned to Li, his hands now gesturing like those of a choir conductor. "This is no longer *your*—" and he waited for the villagers to complete his sentence.

"FAMILY LAND!" all the villagers sang in unison. Then they all laughed.

Li was unaffected by their laughter. "My father served you all these years. Is this how you repay him?"

Feng narrowed his eyes. He had to think of how to teach Li a lesson, once and for all, so his family would never bother him again.

"Continue working," he ordered the villagers, and he took Li aside, out of their sight. He was still holding his plate of desserts.

"Come here, come." He led Li to a corner. Then he held up his plate for her to see. "Look at this plate," he said. Li noticed a half-eaten cake on it, alongside biscuit crumbs. An elaborate dark-blue design adorned the edges of the plate. "This plate has served me for many years," Feng began. "It served my breakfast, lunch, and dinner."

Suddenly, his hands let go of the plate. It dropped to the ground and shattered to pieces. Li looked at the porcelain pieces on the ground, then back at her uncle, with surprise. "Oops. Now it is broken," he said. "It was good while it served me. But now that I have no more use for it, you know where it belongs?" He answered his own question. "In the *garbage!*" He looked at her. "Your father was no different."

Li's nostrils suddenly flared, and her eyes blazed with anger. Her uncle smirked, surprised but pleased that his words were having such an impact. Li had to draw upon every ounce of her restraint to not break his nose right there. She took a breath, reminding herself that only she controlled what she let affect her. Rather than interpret her uncle's words as insults, she decided to take them as a challenge. And she accepted that challenge. Without wasting another second of her time, she turned and left.

As she passed back through the villagers, her uncle called loudly from behind her, "Li! Don't forget to take some food for your mother and sister!" He offered it to her as though she were a beggar.

Without a backward glance, she walked out the gates.

She found the sky orange and the dirt road colored in the same hue. The pathways felt empty. It was as though everyone in the village was at her uncle's house. She looked to the ground beside her. Only her shadow accompanied her, faithfully.

As she kept walking, her mind roamed in its own world. She was the man of the house now. She had to financially support her family. And she had to fulfill her father's wish.

But how? Though monkhood occupied her, it was not an occupation. She had never earned a single coin. Until now, her monastic lifestyle had fulfilled all her core human needs without requiring money. She found food in the Temple garden, and a home in the Temple. She found love among her brother monks and a connection with Mother Nature. In her daily training and meditation, she had the opportunity to grow. And from teaching younger monks, she had the chance to give. In striving to fulfill her potential for growing and giving, she had purpose.

She paused and looked at the vast, verdant farmlands, washed in dying sunlight. Seeing her uncle had sparked in her a new need—one that required lots of money. *But how would she make it?* She had no formal education, and with only the lower-tier jobs open to her, it would be decades before she could afford to buy back her father's former land rights. But failing to do this was not an option. She had to find a way. She racked her brain for answers. All she found were obstacles.

Soon, she reached her family home. When she opened the door, she found Lian stirring dinner on the stove and Mei cutting vegetables. "So how did it go?" Mei asked.

Li looked to her sister, then to her mother. "Keep father's ashes," she said. "I promise that one day, I will get back our family land. And we will bury him there, as he always wished."

Her mother and Mei continued preparing dinner as though nothing of significance had been said. But Li meant her words, and she would see them realized.

CHAPTER 16

The next day, Li returned to live in the Shaolin Temple and headed to the Mahavira Hall, in the seventh courtyard. Stepping into the prayer hall, she stood before three giant golden statues of Buddhas. They were sitting cross-legged and staring at her with sleepy eyes and soft smiles. Enshrined in the middle was the Sakyamuni Buddha, and to its East and West were the Bhaisajyaguru (Medicine) Buddha and the Amitabha (Infinite Light) Buddha. They represented the present, past, and future. Two large maroon pillars flanked Li, each guarded by a giant stone lion.

Li turned her attention to the sand bowl and lit candle on the wooden table before her. With tense shoulders, she picked up three incense sticks. She lit them in the flame and, once they carried wisps of smoke, inserted them in the sand bowl.

Kneeling on the pillow before her, she lowered her head to the ground multiple times. In the background, some monks were chanting, their hypnotic intonations interspersed with the "ting" of a small bell. The stirring voices mixed in the air, threaded with incense.

Resting her forehead on the ground, Li prayed from the depths of her heart. *I need to fulfill my promise.* She squeezed her eyes. *Please, grant me guidance.* The monks' melody moved into her marrow, alleviating the tension in her muscles and mind. *Please, grant me guidance.*

As she rose from the pillow a long time later, her chest felt lighter. She took a deep breath and hoped the guidance would manifest to her in a dream.

That night, while she was asleep, Li's eyes suddenly opened. "That's it!" she gasped. She hadn't had a dream, but an idea had come to her. She hoped her mind would retain it till morning. Turning on her other side, she awaited the sunrise.

The next morning, after training, she ran to the Shaolin Temple tourism office. "So you want to be a tour guide?" an official with a square face and glasses said behind his desk. Li nodded. She knew English and was well versed in stories about the various monuments in the Shaolin Temple. The official smiled. "We don't have many tour guides who can speak both English and Mandarin."

After several days of training, Li received a white shirt, black pants, a nametag, and a job as a part-time tour guide during the monks' afternoon break.

Tourists from around the world visited, and Li would share with them stories of the monuments and landmarks in the Shaolin Temple.

"This creature looks like a turtle." Li pointed to a black marble statue in one courtyard as a group of South American tourists followed. "But it isn't. It has the back of a turtle and the head of a dragon." In a hushed voice, she imparted with a dramatic flair, "They say if you rub its neck, you will gain good health. If you rub its teeth, you will become rich. And if you rub its back, you will live a long life." Then she watched which area each of the tourists rubbed, gleaning from this their priorities in life. One of them stood before the creature, vacillating over where he would rub it. "Of course, you can rub all areas of its body," she said. He laughed and greedily did so.

"This statue here is a favorite among the Chinese." Li gestured to a small marble creature lying like a sphinx by one of the stone staircases. A British couple in their late sixties followed her today. "It eats and eats but does not excrete." The couple frowned, unsure how this was a virtue. "It means you make more and more money without losing it." Now understanding, the couple laughed and nodded. They rubbed the statue's back.

At the end of the tour, the man paid her. "And this is a tip," he said, handing her twenty yuan more.

"Why? What for?" Li asked with surprise.

"You were a really great tour guide," his wife gushed.

"No, no, no," Li waved her hand, refusing the extra money, even though she needed it. "This is my job."

The couple pushed, but she adamantly resisted. Finally, she said, "If you want, you can put it in the Shaolin Temple donation box."

Li showed her next tour group, a cluster of elementary school students, the grounds of the Shaolin training hall. "What do you see?" she asked them.

"There are many pits in the floor," one boy remarked.

"Like giant feet!" another added.

"Correct," she smiled. "There are forty-eight depressions in the floor. These were formed as monks for hundreds of years pounded their feet on the floor while training." She stomped her feet, showing them the various movements the monks would do.

"Whoaaaw," the kids exclaimed as they observed her speed and power.

"Kung Fu skills cannot be acquired in a day, just as these marks were not formed overnight." Li extolled the virtues of patience and perseverance to them. The little kids gasped and clasped their hands.

Li skipped up a stone staircase to what was known as the Snow Pavilion. She looked at the tourist family of four in front of her. "Do you know why Shaolin monks bow *amitofu*, with only their right hand, while other monks around the world bow with two hands?"

"No," the teenage brother and sister said, only now realizing the difference.

"Why?" the father asked.

"Well, it began with Bodhidharma, or as the Chinese called him, Da Mo," Li shared. "He was the first Zen Buddhist monk. He came from India to spread his Buddhism. But because he did not speak Chinese, many people did not like him. He decided then that he would walk all the way to the Shaolin Temple. It took him seven years. By the time he reached here, he was fluent in Chinese and attracted a lot of attention. But still, he refused to teach the Shaolin monks.

"One of the monks, named Shen Guang, persisted in wanting to be Da Mo's disciple. He followed Da Mo for years, standing outside and acting as his bodyguard while Da Mo meditated. Occasionally, he asked Da Mo to teach him, but Da Mo always ignored him. So one winter day, after waiting for more than a decade, Shen Guang grew angry and demanded to know when Da Mo would teach him. Da Mo answered, 'When the snow turns red.'"

She looked at the kids. "In other words, 'Never,'" the boy said.

She raised her brows and continued. "When Shen Guang heard this, he drew the sword he carried in his belt and cut off his left arm. Then he swung the arm around, spilling his blood on the snow. 'Now the snow is red,' he said. 'Now you must teach me.' And impressed by his commitment, Da Mo accepted him as his disciple. So to show respect for Shen Guang's sacrifice, the Shaolin monks today bow with only their right hand."

The family looked at her, amazed.

One sunny afternoon, Li was guiding two American men. One was in his fifties—a short, chubby man with a ruddy complexion. The other was a thin man in his thirties, wearing thick, black-framed glasses. He was filming with a small digital camera as Li led them along a pathway lined with walnut trees.

As a wind blew past them, a rustling noise sounded from one of the branches, followed by a snap. Two walnuts came hurtling toward the older man's head. Li flicked her hands back, then sideways, striking them away. The walnuts rolled harmlessly on the ground.

The men stood agape and exchanged glances. "Your reflexes are fast!" the older man exclaimed.

Li gave a slight bow of the head. She shared that she trained as a Shaolin monk at the Temple.

"Can you do a kick in the air?" the younger one asked. Li nodded. Swiftly, she jumped into the air, performing an elaborate spin kick.

The men gasped. As she landed, they whispered something to one another. Then, the older one turned to Li.

"My name is Steve. I'm a film director," he revealed. "And this is my assistant, Josh." Josh smiled and nodded. "We shoot a lot of action movies and need good stunt doubles. The pay is good, if you're interested."

"Like, two to three thousand dollars for every scene," Josh added, "which is, what…" he paused to calculate. "Twelve to fifteen thousand yuan."

Li's breath caught. But immediately she regained her composure.

Steve pulled his business card from his wallet. "We're based in California and happy to employ skilled stunt doubles. You'd be excellent."

Li took the business card and put it in her back pocket, then carried on with the rest of the tour.

For many nights, while her brother monks were asleep, Li's thoughts kept her awake. She compared what she was getting as a tour guide here to what she could be getting as a stunt double in America. Though she was comfortable in her present job, at this rate it would take decades before she could buy back her family land. *But if I move to America*, she mused, *become a stunt double, and make a couple of movies a year…* Her soul lifted. *I could fulfill my promise in no time!* She wished David were here so he could reassure and advise her. But he had since left the Temple, and she'd had no news of him.

Li turned in bed to face the crescent moon through the window. She had never traveled before, let alone been so far from her family. She did not know what America would be like for her. Gazing at the dark side of the moon, she thought, *I would be leaving home for some unknown place.* It was the uncertainty of what lay ahead that most held her back. The future before her was a dark void, and she would have to toss herself in it, having faith that it would lead to her goals.

Night after night, these thoughts continued to fill her mind. At first, they came as a focused stream. Then into the wee hours, they washed over her in waves, going back and forth between spells of sleep.

But one day, by the time the sky out her window was turning pink, she came to a decision: *If I am truly serious about fulfilling my promise, then I must go.*

That afternoon, she was with her shifu in the vegetable garden. They were picking remnants of their harvest before the winter snowfalls began. Li was kneeling, pulling out soil-covered potatoes and onions and dropping them in a bucket. Her eyes were dry, as she had barely slept for several nights. She yawned.

The shifu looked at her. Then he walked to a large slab of stone and sat.

"Come here," he said, patting the space beside him on the stone.

Li sat by his side. Her eyes gazed at the large gray clouds that stretched beyond. Faint golden light delineated their edges.

Her shifu's voice brought her back. "Is there something bothering you?"

Li had not fully prepared what she would tell her shifu. But sitting beside him, in his peaceful presence, she felt the words naturally flow out. "I want to go to America."

She explained her family's difficult situation after her father's death, and the promise she had made. Grayer clouds were gathering beneath the large ones, swirling and darkening the sky.

Her shifu dropped his gaze to the ground. After a while, he nodded, then got up. He strolled around the garden, hands behind his back. "Look around you, Li."

Li followed his gaze but was unsure where to look.

"Look at the trees, the lake, the sun, the soil, this bucket." He gestured around. "Everything in nature is made of different things: wood, water, fire, earth, metal. They each play a different role." Li waited for him to explain how this related to her. "This wood fuels fire." He motioned to a tree beside him. "The fire forms ashes on the earth; the earth harbors metal; this metal bucket carries water, and this water nourishes the wood. Everything is in harmony—because everything in nature embraces its own nature."

A wind blew, swaying the trees. He turned to her. "Likewise, Li, we are all different. We each have a purpose in this world. But how can you play your part if you do not embrace it to the full? You cannot be the best version of yourself if you are not yourself to begin with." His voice dropped. "No matter where you go or what you do, Li, if you are not yourself, you will never be happy."

Li's heart suddenly skipped. *Why is he saying this?* She did not want to let herself understand his words, but her suspicions whispered: *Has he known all along that I am a girl?* She herself had become oblivious to it over the years. She tried to find confirmation in his eyes.

Thunder suddenly broke, emitting a loud rumble that echoed across the mountain ranges. It startled Li. The first drops of rain came down on their heads, cooling Li's bare scalp.

"Let us go inside for some tea," the shifu said. And as he walked ahead, she followed.

They entered the tearoom, which had pistachio-colored walls. Li took a seat at the wooden table while her shifu prepared tea. Gazing out the window at the dark trees, Li could hear the raindrops pattering down on their branches and remaining leaves. She breathed in the moist air, smelling the soil washed in rain. A second clap of thunder struck, rolling across the sky. This one was accompanied by a massive downpour, spraying the floor and drumming on the roof. Li felt secure inside, content with her sheltered place.

The shifu now set the teapot on the table before them and poured tea in both their cups. Li looked at the aromatic steam rising from hers. Holding it with both hands, she took a sip.

While she was drinking, her shifu went to a large wooden cabinet in the corner of the room. He opened the cabinet door and from a top shelf brought down a small wooden box. Opening the lid, he pulled out a yellow satin pouch. Then, to Li's surprise, he handed it to her.

"What is this?" Li asked, taking it with both hands.

"Open it," the shifu said as he now joined her at the table and took the first sip of his tea.

Li opened the pouch slowly, and her eyes widened. Inside the pouch was a ruby ring. Pulling it out, Li inspected its golden band and the ruby in its center. The gem glowed a deep yet bright red, as though it encased a scintillating flame.

"I've kept this ring with me ever since my father gave it to me as a little boy," her shifu shared. "Now, I want you to have it, Li."

Li looked at her shifu, perplexed. "Why are you giving this to *me*?!"

"You have a long journey ahead of you," he began slowly, "one filled with challenges... Every time you face a challenge, remember this ruby. It would not have become a ruby without intense heat and pressure. Likewise, Li, you will face the heat of the people and the pressure to conform." His eyes locked on hers. "But if you do not struggle through it, you will be no different from an ordinary stone."

As Li looked at her shifu—the radiant compassion and gentle lines on his face—she uttered no words. Instead, a hot tear fell on her cheek. In that one drop of saltwater was an ocean of appreciation. She thought of how her shifu had become like a father to her. He loved her unconditionally and accepted her without judgment, making her feel whole whenever she was around him. Over the years, he had trained her to grow strong, encouraged her when she was good, never told her she was bad but instead always showed her the right way. The silence that hung between them was not empty; rather, it carried the fullness and depth of her emotions better than any words.

CHAPTER 17

Los Angeles, USA

Li stepped into the dimly lit motel room. The sound of a rattling old AC emanated from one corner. *I am in America*, she had to remind herself, almost unable to believe she was standing on this country's land. She dropped her backpack on the bed. Then she crossed the sticky tan carpet to get to the window. The curtains were milky white, dulled with grey. As she pulled them aside, dust billowed into the air. She heaved up the window, and the hot humidity of the night latched onto her face.

Puddles on the ground reflected the orange streetlights. They dimly lit an alleyway, but the darkness still obscured the graffiti on the brick walls. A man with his hands deep in his pockets trudged by and spat on the sidewalk. Police sirens sounded. There was chatter and laughter. Someone screamed. Li stepped back and closed the window, but the sounds permeated the glass.

She opened the squeaking closet and caught her reflection in the body-length mirror that hung behind its door. She was wearing Mei's earth-colored floral dress, and her hair had grown into a short crop. She had decided to follow her shifu's advice and embrace her own nature.

Shaolina, her sister's voice sounded in her ear. That was the female name Mei had chosen for her, inspired by Li's identity as a Shaolin monk. *A feminine name and a dress? Is that all it takes?* Her whole life, she had been raised as a male. *What does it mean to be a woman? To be female?* she wondered.

She closed the closet door and sat on the bed. Her backpack was all she had brought. Pulling it to her lap, she embraced it and thought about her mother. The first time Li had shared her decision to find work in America, and to do so as a woman, her mother had disapproved. But Li persisted until she agreed—on one condition: Li had to leave the village as a man. With Hai gone, they could not afford to be further weakened by others knowing they had no males in the family. Li had agreed.

Now, she unzipped her backpack and drew out a red pouch. A slim roll of hundred dollar bills lay inside. Li unfurled them. Her thumbs grazed along the bills as she began to count.

This was all her family's money, here in her hands. Lian had sold her wedding ring and given Li their savings to cover her initial expenses. Tears formed. *Mother,* her mind's voice spoke with resoluteness, *I will not let you down.*

The next morning arrived. Li stood before a large, blocky, beige building. On its front were a large logo, and shiny silver letters proclaiming: Film Productions. She walked through the sliding glass door and was greeted with a rush of cool air, infused with a strong citrus perfume. The source of the perfume was a reception desk.

There, a blond woman was chattering on the phone. Li stared at the golden curls framing her protruding cheekbones, and at her dark, thick eyelashes. Her nose was a long, thin line pointing down a heavily made-up face and towards pouty lips. Her light-blue dress revealed cleavage. Li had never seen such a woman.

The woman finished her conversation and shifted her icy blue eyes to Li. She scanned Li up and down, from her bare face and barely grown hair to her flat chest and outdated, ill-fitting dress. "How can I help you?" she said, sounding annoyed.

Li pulled out the business card that the director had handed to her and placed it on the counter. "I want to see Director Stevenson, please."

The woman didn't glance at her card. "Do you have an appointment?"

"Umm... I don't—"

"Then I'm sorry." She didn't look sorry. "You can't see the director without an appointment."

Li's heart thrummed in her chest. "Can I make appointment?"

"I'm sorry," the woman repeated. "The director's very busy."

Li felt her body heat rise and her face redden. "But I came all the way from China to see him. I have to see him," she pushed.

"I need you to leave now," the woman said.

"But, I need—"

"I told you, he's busy!" the woman raised her voice.

A man in his thirties paced over to them. He was slim, of average height, and wore glasses with thick black rims that framed his blue eyes.

"What's going on here?" he asked.

"Sorry for disturbing you," the woman turned to him. "I explained to this woman that the director is busy." She gestured to Li. "But she doesn't seem to understand."

Upon catching sight of the man's face, Li's eyes lit. It was the assistant director, Josh, who had toured with the director at the Shaolin Temple. She was saved.

Josh turned to Li, his voice calm. "How can I help you?" he started. But then he paused. Pointing a finger to her, he said, "Hey, do I know you? You look very familiar." As Li was opening her mouth to answer, he let out, "Ah! I remember!" He narrowed his eyes. "Are you related to that monk who gave us a tour?"

It suddenly hit Li that she had been a male monk in their eyes when she gave them the tour. She looked down at her floral dress. Her stomach lurched.

"He was my brother!" she stammered. "He told me that you're hiring stunt doubles. I'm also very good at martial arts."

"We'll be the judge of that," Josh said. "But give us one moment." He raised a finger. "Let us first check if there are openings." He turned to the receptionist. "Can you pull up the schedule?" She clicked on the keyboard and Josh came around the desk to look at her screen.

Li could see the screen light reflected off his glasses as he scrolled down, his eyes darting from left to right. She held her breath, hoping that any second, he would stop mid-screen, gasp, and call out an opening.

He sighed and faced her. "I'm sorry, but we don't have any job openings for stunt doubles right now."

The tile floors were spinning beneath Li's feet. She was incredulous. "But Director Stevenson said you shoot a lot of action movies, and you need good stunt doubles," she persisted. She had hung on his every word.

"Yeah," Josh shrugged his shoulders. "Unfortunately, right now, we don't have any openings. But leave your phone number. We'll contact you if a slot opens up."

Li didn't have a phone, so she put down her motel's phone number. As she walked out the door, her head felt too heavy to lift. She still could not believe what had transpired.

The next day, Li asked the motel receptionist whether there had been a call for her. There was no call. The day after that, she checked again, with the same eagerness, only to get the same answer. She checked again a day later. Still the answer was the same.

During her time waiting, Li was like a captive in her motel room, frozen, focused on waiting for the call. To save money, she ate only instant noodles from the corner convenience story and austerely limited her other purchases. Still, every day she waited, the roll of bills in her pouch got thinner and thinner. She had to get that call quickly so she could move on.

As she sat alone on the motel bed, paranoia was a frequent visitor. Maybe they had called, but the motel receptionist hadn't answered. Or perhaps in that moment at the reception desk, she had been blinded by panic and had written down the wrong phone number.

Growing desperate, Li decided to return to the director's office. But upon seeing her, the blond receptionist said, "We don't have an opening," and turned her away.

Walking back to the motel, Li felt more and more naïve. And stupid. She had left everything, come all this way, believing there was an opportunity for her. She thought of the promise she had made to restore her family's land rights. Her mother had entrusted to her their life savings, believing she would save their lives.

But in a matter of two weeks, her pouch was nearly empty, and she had to leave the motel.

CHAPTER 18

With no place to stay and no destination in mind, Li carried her backpack and began walking. She ventured far past the now-familiar neighborhood around her motel, walking and walking until she entered a place of glimmering shops, tall, slender palm trees, and wide, spotless sidewalks. An assortment of brightly colored cars lined the streets, winking in the sunlight.

A white car pulled up and parked outside a store. As the back door opened, a long leg ending in a red high-heeled sandal stepped out. Li watched as the owner of that leg emerged: a woman in a pink mini-dress and masked with makeup. Without looking left or right, the woman walked straight into the store. Li could not even look into the woman's eyes; she seemed to be on another level.

As the store doorman continued to hold the door open, a suit-clad, middle-aged man emerged. As the sun greeted his face, he donned sunglasses and paced towards a glossy black car. Li's eyes were caught by the giant golden watch on his wrist before he got into his car and drove off.

Li looked through the shop windows at sparkling jewelry, handbags, and clothes that hugged the mannequins' bodies. She felt disdain. These stores advertised confidence and happiness. People unable to earn them went in to purchase them. But Li told herself that these things could not be bought. She thought of her shifu's teachings: pleasure is not the same as happiness. You can get pleasure from the external environment, but it is as fleeting as the external world is changing. True happiness is a state of being. It comes from within. It is the lens within us that colors the world outside us.

"Don't stand here." A man's voice interrupted Li's thoughts. She saw that the doorman was looking at her sternly. "Go away!" Li continued onward, walking and walking.

Just as the sun was setting, she crossed over to a darker side of the city. There, she found a string of shuttered shops. The store windows were cloudy. Rather than displaying products, they showed "No Cash In Store" signs. The only things that sparkled were the shards of glass scattered on the sidewalks. People wore basic clothes and bare faces. As Li walked, she felt a dozen pairs of eyes on her. Alongside, some men sat on newspapers on the pavement, sharing a cigarette. Another used the sidewalk curb as his pillow. The pace here was slow. People who passed by each other on the streets recognized one another and paused to converse.

By the time it was dark, she had reached a quiet, dim alley. Her stomach felt light from emptiness, and her feet were heavy from weariness. Her legs buckled beneath her, and she sat on the ground, back against a brick wall.

She looked up into the starless sky. Dark clouds were brewing. She had always wandered the mountains at night. The darkness had blanketed her in comfort and uncovered to her the stars. This darkness was different. For the first time, she feared its eeriness.

It was the darkness of the future she feared most. She was lost—and she had lost her family's savings. Her trembling hand covered her mouth, and thick tears blinded her. She tried to take long, deep breaths. But there was a swelling in her chest. Like a bubble, it expanded outward and outward, constricting her breathing, crushing her lungs. In her mind, she was screaming out loud. In the alley, her sobs were barely audible. *If only I had enough money, I'd buy a plane ticket and return home.*

Opening her backpack, she pulled out her shifu's ring. Though the alley was dim, the ruby glowed deep red. As she touched it, her shifu's words rang in her ears.

She sniffed and wiped her eyes. The bubble in her chest seemed to deflate, and she could breathe a little more easily. She took in a deep breath, and let it out. This was not the end of the road, only a roadblock. Her goal—restoring her family's land rights—was still there. Just because her original means of getting there had not worked did not mean she would give up. *I just have to find another way.*

Thunder suddenly struck.

Slipping the ring on her finger, Li rose to her feet and put on her backpack. She had to find shelter before it rained. She stepped forward. But somehow, she wasn't moving forward.

Someone was pulling her backpack.

She wheeled around to find a towering man with broad shoulders and a dark face. "Give me your bag." His voice was deep. Then he spotted the ruby ring on her finger. "Give me that ring."

Li clenched her fist and stepped back. She heard movements from around her.

"Ring?"

"Someone's got jewelry?"

Four men of varying sizes emerged from the darkness on both sides of Li. Upon seeing them, Li quickly placed her back to the wall and shifted into her fighting stance. Her eyes surveyed each one of them.

"Guys! Hold on! Hold on! You don't wanna mess with this," one of them raised his hands. "This is *Bruce Lee* here!"

The men broke into hysterics. "Hey, Bruce Lee!" one of them called. "Why are you wearing a dress?"

Li clenched her fist.

Staring at Li's ferocious eyes, the thin man among them was galvanized. He let out a shrill cry and charged towards her. Immediately, Li kicked his kneecap, halting him, and popped a punch to his nose.

The man screeched in pain and staggered backwards, holding his nose. As he withdrew his hand, he found it covered in red. "It's bleeding!" he exclaimed incredulously. "She gave me a bloody nose!"

The other men exchanged glances. *This fighter is for real.* The large one looked around him and found a scrap of metal pipe on the ground. As he picked it up, it scraped along the asphalt. "I'll teach you," he snarled, approaching Li with heavy steps. In the dark, the whites of his eyes gleamed.

Li narrowed her eyes. She was measuring his height and reach, and the distance between the men. A flurry of actions already filled her mind.

"GUYS! STOP!" A woman's voice suddenly sounded from the back. A skinny brown girl in her late teens ran and stood between Li and the men. "Shame on you!" She eyed each one. "Five grown men fighting one woman!"

Shame suddenly seared into them, and a hint of civility returned to their faces. "Doesn't fight like a woman," one of them muttered.

The girl shot daggers at him. "This isn't just any woman. She's my friend!"

The large one held the back of his head. "Aysha, dat's your friend?" He tossed the metal pipe to the side with a clang. "I didn't know dat."

"It's all right," she said. Then she quickly grabbed Li by the arm and led her out of the alley.

Once they were far from the men, Li spoke. "Thank you for helping me, Aysha. My name is Shaolina."

Aysha nodded. Li felt a drop of water on her face, then another. A few seconds later, the rain began coming down heavily.

"Do you have a place to stay?" Aysha turned to Li, rain pouring over her head and face. She could pick out those who were new to the streets, not from their cleaner clothes or hygiene, but mostly from the uncertainty written on their faces and in their bodies.

"Uh, no," Li murmured.

"Then let me take you to my place."

Quickly, Aysha leading, the women jogged toward the end of another dimly lit alley. "That's my home!" Aysha said under the roaring rain. To Li's surprise, she was pointing to a rundown van. It was a light-blue Volkswagen with flat tires.

Aysha heaved open the van door and gestured for Li to enter.

Li ducked her head and got inside. Aysha joined her and pulled the door closed, then locked it. The rain rapped on the hood and streamed down the windows.

Li looked around in the van. Even though it was dark, she could see clothes, blankets, cans, bottles, and other objects scattered in the back seats. The leather of the seat beside her was ripped, and fragments of sponge poked out. Li turned her attention to Aysha, still thinking about what had just happened. "Those men—you know them?"

Aysha looked at her. "Yeah," she said. "That big man, Boomer, is the leader of a gang." She paused. "From time to time, he gives me some money. You don't know how much you need it, that extra help, until you get sick."

"Why does he give you money?" Li asked.

Aysha shrugged. "I heard there's a man called Robin who gives it to him so he can give it out to people like us on the streets."

As Aysha spoke, Li examined her. She looked so young. Li wondered what she was doing alone on the streets. "So where is your family?" she asked.

Aysha felt like someone had blown the dust off a long-forgotten, deep-hidden memory. She blinked. "No one's asked about my life in a long time," she said, her voice suddenly raspy. "I uhh—" she glanced again at Li. There was something about her presence that made Aysha feel safe. There was no judgment in her eyes. It was as though this stranger's chest was open to her, holding space for her in her heart.

Aysha leaned back, gazing at the seat in front as though it were a projector screen for the memories that now flashed through her mind. "I was living with my family a few years ago," she began. "Father was an alcoholic. He always beat my mother, older brother, and I. Then when I was sixteen, my mother passed. So my brother was like the parent in my life. When my father kept beating us, my brother couldn't take it anymore. One day, they had a big fight. 'We're leaving! This isn't a way to live,' he told me after the fight. He took my hand and we left.

"Then all was good for a while," Aysha exhaled. "My brother joined the military. He would pay for our small rental apartment. Sometimes, I felt lonely. But he reminded me that he was always with me. He stood by my side; he supported me to continue high school. Every day, I thanked God that I had him. Then one day"—she paused, looking to the roof of the van, trying to hold back her tears. She resumed, her voice hoarse now. "One day, I came back from school and got a call that my brother had been killed in an explosion while deployed." Aysha clenched her teeth and looked away.

Li's eyes were filled with sympathy.

Aysha swallowed and continued her story. "I had no family left other than my father, so I returned to his house. But when I got there, I found a different family living there. My father had sold the house and moved away. I never found him."

"You—you need family." She gestured with her hands. "In, in this world, only family supports you all the way, no matter what. You know what I mean?" She looked at Li. "You make mistakes, we all make mistakes... but most people have family to pull them back up. I didn't." She bit her fingers, pulling a bit of skin off her thumb. "So after that, everything sort of piled on top of me. I got caught up in alcohol and drugs. I dropped out of school. Now, I'm homeless."

They sat in silence. The raindrops rapped on the roof less frequently now.

Aysha then dropped her hand to her lap. "So what brings you here?"

Suddenly, Li's stomach rumbled. "Sorry!" She blushed. "I haven't eaten since morning."

Aysha looked out the window. Droplets sat on the glass, and the puddles outside no longer rippled. The rain had subsided. She smiled at Li. "I'm hungry too. Let's grab something to eat."

She slid open the door and hopped outside, then led

Li towards a fast-food restaurant. "There's always free food here."

Li tilted her head back. She didn't know that restaurants gave away free food. Then she saw Aysha open a dumpster in front of the restaurant, plunge her hand inside, and pull out a half-eaten burger.

"This is a good size!"

"No, no, no," Li waved her hands. "I have a bit of money left." She reached for her backpack zipper to pull out her pouch. "I can buy us some food."

"If you have money left, save every penny of it, girl," Aysha said. "While you can get free food from here, take it."

Li's heart sank. She knew Aysha had a point. A part of her yearned to detach from her body and fly away—away from this place, away from this country, away from this life. But her stomach continued to rumble, returning her back to her body.

"It's okay," Aysha said with a soft voice, "you'll get used to it." She passed the burger towards her. "Just cut out the bitten part."

With cinched lips, Li took it.

Aysha fished out another partial burger for herself, then sat with her back against the dumpster. With nowhere else to go, Li slowly slid down to join her. The neon red lights of the restaurant contrasted with the black night sky reflected off the rain puddles. A few people walked past them.

Li hadn't realized just how hungry she was until she took her first bite. A vegetarian, she ate only the bun.

"So tell me," Aysha spoke while chewing, "what brings you here?"

Li shared her family's situation in China, and the promise she'd made to lift them out of their situation. When Aysha remarked that her English was really good, Li told her about her childhood friend David, who had taught her.

Aysha felt the need to help her. There was something inspiring about this girl, who was as beaten down and broke as she was, yet still fighting for a way to raise herself. "If you want," she said with her mouth full, "you can stay with me."

CHAPTER 19

Buzzzzzzzzzz. A fly was hovering near Li's ears. She flicked her hands back. The sudden movement sent drops of sweat rolling down her face. She peered through heavy eyelids. *Where am I?* Torn, milky-colored leather seats greeted her. Still lying down, she turned her head the other way. Scenes from yesterday replayed in her mind. She was not sure whether they were real or part of a dream. "Aysha?" she called. Her throat was raspy from dehydration. She sat up, then shifted and looked over to the long seat in front of her. Aysha was not there. Only some blankets and clothes lay jumbled on it.

Li shifted to the edge of her seat and slid open the van door. As she walked along the shaded alleyway, she spotted Aysha at the open end, leaning on a building. She was holding a short cigarette between her thumb and forefinger, smoking.

"Aysha!" she called.

Aysha turned. In daylight, Li could see the curly, dark-brown hair that fell on her shoulders. She had soft, light-brown skin, full lips, and hazel eyes. She looked to be in her early twenties.

"Hey, sleepyhead," Aysha replied.

She took a drag on her cigarette. It was deep, almost like Li's meditation breaths. Then she exhaled a cloud of smoke. "Come on, let's find something to eat," she said. She tossed her stub of a cigarette on the ground and stepped on it.

Aysha led Li down a street overrun with tents and makeshift shelters. Lining the building walls were bright and dull tents, blue tarps, and black garbage bags. Some people's faces peered from under these covers. Men and women were sitting on chairs, from plastic chairs to office chairs, outside their tents. One had a barbecue grill in front of him, the smoke from it mixing with the smoke of his cigarette.

A tall, shirtless black man loped down the street, and another was bent over, sorting through his stuff. Bikes passed them. A man pissed in a white bucket, then dumped its contents in the trash. A woman washed her clothes in the gushing of a yellow fire hydrant.

Aysha then led Li down a more crowded street. In front of them, people pushed trolleys overflowing with their belongings. On Li's side, many squatted, their backs against metal shutters, gazing at her. There were people talking, sometimes yelling, to themselves, shaking their heads, gesturing with their arms. A woman sprayed juice from her mouth onto an onlooker. Another was curled up in a fetal position, rolling side to side, groaning in agony.

A shoeless man trotted by them, nearly stepping on the shards of glass littering the sidewalks. "Who stole my shoes?!" he yelled. The sounds of passing cars, shouts, and dog barks filled the hot air, and the stench of urine and feces was ubiquitous. A few bodies lay on a heap of blankets, boxes, and trash. Insects crawled from the pile.

All this was against the backdrop of numerous gleaming skyscrapers. It was the starkest of contrasts for Li—some living high in the clouds, and others hard on the ground. Li wondered whether the difference in these people's humanity was so stark as to merit such disparity in their lived realities.

"You see that man?" Aysha pointed, turning to Li. "He lost his wife and children in a car accident. Then he lost his mind, then his job, and then his home. That guy," she pointed to one walking down the other side of the street, wearing an army cap and a camo jacket, "is a veteran. They were taking so long to treat his pain that he went to the streets for heroine to numb himself. He got trapped here."

Li listened to Aysha tell the stories of the various homeless people she knew—the hustlers, the hassled, the rebels, the junkies, the sick, the mentally ill, the unfortunate. They each had a story: a tragedy, a family breakup, neglect, abuse, unemployment, eviction, a mistake, the loss of loved ones, the loss of self, and more. Aysha explained that not all the homeless were substance abusers or mentally ill. And while a few had already been dealing with mental illness and substance abuse issues, which contributed to their homelessness, others had developed these issues only after becoming homeless. It was hard to face the streets sober.

Aysha told her it was a vicious cycle, like a hurricane that grew thicker and thicker as it picked up more issues and became more intractable over time. Even the calm at the eye of the storm was a false one. Some swept out of homelessness found themselves sucked back in. Those trying to climb out fell deeper still. Various issues kept spinning around them, trapping them. Li realized how quickly and easily one could fall into homelessness, and how difficult it was to get out. She yearned to prevent herself from falling too deep, being swallowed whole by the vortex.

Aysha kept talking about people clinging to life on a day-by-day basis, but her voice now faded into the background. Li's thoughts took her back to the monks at the Shaolin Temple. They often had even fewer possessions than these homeless on the streets. Yet they were content. Li wondered what the difference was.

As the sun arced through the sky, Aysha showed Li key areas around the city: soup kitchens, thrift shops, public libraries, parks, places where she could nap unbothered, public recreation facilities to slip into for a free shower, and street corners to avoid. Li was grateful to have the streetwise Aysha.

Later in the day, Aysha introduced Li to some of her friends. They all settled by a tent, and the friends shared their pizza with them. After eating, they began smoking a cocktail of drugs. Aysha passed some to Li, but she declined.

"Thank you for the food," Li said.

One of Aysha's friends, a man with chocolate skin and a scruffy beard, laughed and sat back. "Don't thank me, thank Robin Hood." He leaned forward. "You know who Robin Hood is?" Li shook her head. "He's a hero. He and his band of 'outlaws' take from the rich and give to the poor."

"Most of the time, it's the rich who steal from the poor," another of Aysha's friends added, "they're just more polished about it." He was in his early thirties, with frosty-blonde hair, copper eyes, and a faint mustache. He rambled on about corporate greed and the systematic unfairness of the world, taking from those who have less and giving to those who have more. "Those better-off people call us pests, but they're the parasites."

The scruffy old man leaned back again and stared at the large buildings in the background. He took a drag, then exhaled. "Yup," he chuckled. "Thank the Lord we still got people like Robin Hood."

After everyone had fallen silent, they turned to Li. "So how'd you end up here? What's your story?" the second one questioned her.

Li felt uncomfortable explaining. The world was a storm of multilayered, multidimensional, incoherent stimuli, and the simple act of creating a coherent story out of it involved piecing together certain events, interpreting them in a certain way, and ignoring others. She could piece together the events of her life to create any story she wanted. So to expend energy and create a story of how she'd ended up homeless seemed demoralizing. She did not intend to stay here.

"I'm still writing my story," she said. Aysha's friends looked at her, confused, but didn't ask for an explanation. They continued smoking.

That night, there was a metallic-sounding *thump* on the van door. Aysha sat bolt upright. Someone had knocked a can against her vehicle.

"Aysha, what is it?" Li whispered from the front seat as she slowly awoke.

"*Shhh!*"

Aysha had placed cans and old newspapers outside her van so she could hear anyone approaching. Now she heard a shuffling of steps on the newspapers. She peered through the window. A large, heavy figure was staggering in the darkness.

Fear gripping her heart, she ducked down and hissed to Li, "Lie down! Don't let him think there's anyone inside."

The harsh note of fear in her voice chased away Li's sleepiness. Quickly, she slipped down from her seat and knelt in the van's leg area. She could hear the shuffling feet come closer.

The man suddenly began shaking the van.

Aysha let out a shriek of fright before she quickly muffled it. The shaking ceased. The man pressed his forehead against the glass, vicious eyes darting around inside the van.

Aysha pressed her body tighter to the floor, as though hoping to become one with it. She didn't dare flinch a muscle or exhale a breath. To her relief, the man lifted his forehead off the glass.

Then there was no noise. No movement. The only sound was her heartbeat hammering in her chest and pounding in her ears.

"Do you think he left?" Li whispered.

"*Shhhhhhhh.*"

They sat in silent darkness for what seemed like an eternity. Li didn't know when she could let down her guard and relax again. Her friend's hunched shoulders and tenseness told her this wasn't the end of it. Li could not imagine spending every night on the streets like this, on guard while she tried to sleep.

Bang.

They jumped. The sound came from the other door, as the man had circled around. Now he was attacking the van again while yelling obscenities. He was kicking the door and pounding his fist against the window.

Aysha squeezed her eyes and held her breath, praying the old window would not break. Li gritted her teeth, vacillating on whether she should just get out and stop him.

As he was pounding on the window, his breathing became ragged and heavy. He grew tired and stopped.

Suddenly, the door handle began rattling violently as he tried to get inside.

Then they heard another man shout in the distance. Their assailant stopped, and they heard his footsteps fading away. Aysha sagged.

"He left! Thank God!" she exhaled. "We were lucky he didn't break in. He probably would've killed us!"

"He was lucky he didn't break in. I would've taught him a lesson," Li asserted.

Aysha furrowed her brows, studying her strange friend. "Shaolina, if you beat him, he'll come the next day. With ten of his friends! And then they'll definitely kill us. Our lives have no value here."

Li didn't want to gamble with her life on the streets. Her family at home was depending on her. She needed to find a job and get out of here.

CHAPTER 20

When the sun rose, Li went straight out to search for a job. She put on a plain, collared shirt and jeans that Aysha had loaned her. She sniffed herself, hoping she didn't stink too badly. With her fingers, she combed her short hair. A renewed sense of urgency washed through her, and she set out. She visited every store on the block, from the shops and fast-food chains to the grocery stores. Then she tried the next block and the one after that. She did this for one week after another. But all of them turned her down.

Late one morning, as Li was walking down a street, she felt the sun hot on her head. Pearls of sweat rolled down her back. Ahead, glinting in the sunlight, was a wide set of marble steps that led to a large bank. Fatigued, Li decided to take a break on the edge of these steps. She sat and watched the legs of people, in formal suit pants and dresses, pass up and down. Every time someone entered or exited the building, the glass sliding door behind her opened, emitting a rush of cool air that brushed against her back.

Drawn to the cool air, Li entered the building. A security guard by the entrance eyed her. She smiled and he didn't say anything. Li had never seen a bank this large before. She wandered. There was a series of counters, and people were chatting to the bank tellers behind them. Cash and slips of paper passed between them. Monitors beeped. Footsteps clicked on the polished floor. Keyboards clacked. Elevator doors clunked. She imagined what it would be like to work in a polished place like this. No, she shook the thought from her mind. That would never happen, she didn't have the credentials. *I'd better leave before I get kicked out.*

Suddenly, two armed, dark-clad figures charged through the bank entrance. Almost instinctively, Li slipped into a side corridor. She pressed her back against the wall.

BANG! BANG!

Gunshots!

"GET DOWN! I SAID GET DOWN OR I'LL SHOOT YOU!" a man's raspy voice yelled. There were screams, then a third gunshot silenced them.

Cold sweat breaking out around her hairline, Li peered around the corner. All the customers and employees were down on the floor, their hands covering their heads. Others cowered under some benches.

Only the two dark figures were standing. They were fully dressed in black, from their masks and shirts to their pants and shoes. One of them was guarding the door. His eyes swept across the floor of prone bodies, ready to shoot anyone who dared raise their head.

"GET DOWN!" he yelled. The people remaining partially upright whimpered and obeyed.

The second masked man leaped over the counter and went about searching for something. He pointed his gun towards any teller who looked or stood in his way. Then he disappeared through a door at the other end.

Li shifted her gaze back to the first armed man. A body lay directly behind him. She narrowed her eyes. Suddenly, her heartbeat thundered in her ears. It was the security guard she had seen earlier. Now he was on his stomach, a pool of blood spreading beneath him. Li clenched her fist. She wouldn't let them get away with this.

"Move to the corner!" The man swept his gun across the crowd, herding them into a manageable cluster. "Move, *move!*" The people crawled and huddled.

Li flattened herself against the corridor wall, her mind racing through various scenarios and outcomes. *What to do? What to do?* The second she stepped out, they would shoot. No matter how much Shaolin training she had, against a gun she was just as vulnerable as anyone else. Here, she was safe. Out there, she would recklessly risk and probably lose her life. But against the background of their cries, she could not bear to stand idly by.

"Shut up!" the gunman yelled.

Biting her lip, Li glanced out again.

The gunman was now marching towards a woman at the front of the crowd, who was crying. She was crouched over her knees, horror filling her face as he approached.

141

"Please don't kill me," she sobbed. The man leveled his gun at her.

I have to do something now. Li leapt to the side, in his plain sight.

"HEY!" she yelled.

"What?" The man whipped his head towards Li and saw an Asian woman with short hair, a wrinkled white shirt, and outdated mom jeans. He trained his gun on her.

Li's stomach leapt. She lowered slightly and presented the side of her shoulder, rendering herself as narrow a target as possible.

"YOU! GET DOWN!" he ordered.

Li moved to one side, then the other, unpredictably, while advancing closer to him.

The man tried to follow her with his gun. "STOP MOVING!" he yelled, clearly unsettled.

Suddenly, he fired.

But Li had lowered herself beneath the line of fire, diving into a tuck-and-roll towards him. While rolling, with one of her legs she kicked the gun out of his hand. It flew to the side and clattered on the floor. Gasps sounded from the huddled crowd.

She rose and with the momentum of her entire twisting body, struck his jaw.

All consciousness left the man. Standing straight, he fell back, his skull slamming against the floor. Some people cheered.

Li snatched his gun and scurried to the opposite wall.

She edged towards the door where the other armed man had gone.

Footsteps sounded from the staircase behind that door. It then opened, and the second armed man appeared with a full sack. Alarm filled his eyes as he beheld Li. Before he could shoot, she thrust his armed hand to the ceiling. She moved in tight. They wrestled over his weapon, Li twisting his wrist and controlling his elbow so the gun now pointed at him. Under the pressure of the arm lock, he softened his grip. Li snatched the gun and with its back end, socked his temple, knocking him out.

The moment he collapsed, several individuals from the huddled crowd approached and held the gunman down. One removed a necktie, which they used to tie the man's hands. Others had done the same to the second fallen robber.

A few minutes later, a wailing siren sounded, announcing the arrival of police and ambulances. Some people let out cheers of relief, while others hugged each other and cried. Officers swarmed the bank, some detaining the two collapsed criminals and others questioning the witnesses. The security guard, still breathing, was swiftly removed on the stretcher.

After Li had finished talking to one of the officers, a short, middle-aged man in a dark-blue suit approached. He clasped Li's hands and introduced himself as the bank manager, then thanked her profusely for saving them. "We'd like to show our appreciation somehow. What can we do for you?"

Li yearned to tell him, "Nothing," to let the act be a positive in the universe, not cancelled out by any reward in return. But she badly needed money and a job. And with her fruitless record of job seeking, she knew that this moment was perhaps her only chance.

She hesitated.

"I—I'm looking for a job," she said.

The man laughed. "Okay, tomorrow, come back here before noon. Bring your documents and ID, and we'll see what we can do."

The next day, as Li entered the bank, she found a woman with curly auburn hair, a white blouse, pearl earrings, and a black pencil skirt standing by the entrance.

"Hi!" the woman's eyes lit up as they rested on Li. "My name's Stacy." She reached to shake Li's hand. "I've been waiting for you. The CEO asked me to take you to his office."

They got into an elevator, and Stacy pressed the top button. They rode up so quickly that Li's ears popped, but still it took what seemed to her a long time. Finally, the elevator slowed and came to a stop.

As the doors opened and Li stepped into the CEO's office, her mouth gaped. The office was a large expanse of white-carpeted floor, mahogany tables, leather seats, and floor-to-ceiling windows. But what especially caught her attention was the panoramic view of the city. Standing on the soft, snowy carpet above this scene, she felt like she was on a cloud.

"Please, may I have your documents and ID?" Stacy said gently. Li handed to her the paperwork she had brought. Stacy took it with both hands. "Thank you. Please, have a seat." She motioned for Li to sit in a nearby leather sofa. "He'll be with you shortly." And she disappeared.

Li lowered herself slowly onto white leather. It was so pristine, she feared making it dirty. Alone now, she looked at the wide expanse. She felt both a flutter of nervousness and a tickle of anticipation turning in her stomach. She was not sure what to expect.

Soon, from a large wooden door emerged a tall, slim man. He looked to be in his early sixties. He had silver combed back hair and a light gray suit and was holding a file. Li immediately stood up.

"Shaolina!" he greeted, his voice warm and pleasant, and he held out his hand as he approached her. Li shook it. "I must say, I am very impressed by what you did yesterday." She could see the admiration in his twinkling light-brown eyes. "Please, sit down."

He sat behind his large desk. Then he opened the file and took a moment to glance at the paper inside. "I looked at your résumé," he began.

Li's face lifted into a light smile.

"No formal schooling," he spoke. "No recommendation letter. No relevant work experience."

With every "no," Li felt her spirits sink lower and lower. This was like every other place she had applied.

She dropped her head and shifted her feet to the side of her seat, ready for him to tell her to stand up and leave.

"But what good are any of these," he continued, "if a school doesn't teach you compassion, if a résumé doesn't reflect your integrity, if a reference doesn't see you in times of extreme duress?"

Li looked up at him, more confusion than dejection filling her eyes now.

"Yesterday, you showed me what these papers could not. We've decided to place you in our security team, to train our security guards to be more effective. I think you have a lot to offer."

As Li absorbed the words, a smile spread on her shock-parted lips. "Thank you! Thank you, sir!" When she finally found her voice, it was filled with appreciation.

"You can expect to start the job in a couple of weeks. First, we have to process your paperwork."

Li rose to her feet and bowed her head. "Thank you so much!"

"One moment, we're not done here yet," the man spoke. He opened his desk drawer and produced a white envelope, which he handed to her.

Li took it, wondering what could be inside.

"We've decided to grant you this monetary award as well. If you like, we can open a bank account for you here. Stacy would be delighted to help you with the process."

As Li walked back out of his office after they'd exchanged farewells, Stacy greeted her. She explained the paperwork and process Li had to go through to open her bank account. Then she noted the white envelope in Li's hand. "Once you open your account, we can deposit that check," she said. Li curiously opened the envelope, and found a check for several thousand dollars. Never had she seen this amount of money before. A wide smile spread to her face, and her heart thrummed with elation and incredulity. Stacy then escorted her down to the ground floor.

When the elevator doors pinged opened, Li was suddenly met by a swarm of reporters and camera flashes. She blinked and stepped back. But the elevator doors clunked behind her, making her feel trapped. The cameras kept flashing. A reporter shoved a microphone into her face.

"Shaolina, what made you risk your life and confront the criminals?"

Li hesitated, unsure how to answer. "Uh, anyone in my place would have done something to help," she said. The reporter smiled.

"Shaolina! Shaolina!" another reporter drew her attention. "Those were some amazing fighting skills! Where did you learn martial arts?"

"From the Shaolin Temple in China," she replied.

"Why did you come here from China?" another reporter pressed.

Li was uncomfortable. She didn't feel like narrating her life story to strangers. Never before the center of attention, she wanted only to escape from the sea of reporters.

She turned to Stacy at her side and whispered, "Can I leave now?"

Stacy understood. She raised her hands and declared to the reporters, "That's enough for now. Thank you." She then moved ahead through the reporters, clearing a path for Li to exit.

As Li stepped out of the bank, she could not believe the opportunity that had so unexpectedly come to her. The sky was bright blue, and the sun's rays kissed her skin. She felt a warm tingling on her arms. She smiled as though her pressed lips were struggling to contain the cry of joy she held inside.

She started with a skip to her steps. Everything appeared as a pop of color. She passed a line of glistening cars stuck in traffic, hearing not the honking of their horns but the upbeat music emanating from one of their radios. Without realizing it, her head was bobbing to the tunes. Life was smiling upon her, and she smiled back. The side streets were lined with wispy trees, and as their leaves fluttered in the breeze, they seemed to be laughing with her. As she looked up to the tall skyscrapers ahead, she did not feel tiny. Rather, with her elevated spirit, she felt like she too could scrape the sky. She felt like a person who, after dragging along for months, had hopped on the express train to success. Suddenly, she was no longer wandering aimlessly but going places. Suddenly, she had a path for reaching her dreams.

She passed by boutique stores with their colorfully clad mannequins on display. Soon, she could purchase one of these dresses, if she wanted. *If* she wanted. But no, thank you. Simply the thought of her new purchasing power pleased her. It was a measure of her progress, of her moving a step closer to fulfilling her promise to her family. As she looked at the store windows again, she saw not the mannequins on display but her smiling reflection.

She then passed sidewalk cafés with caramel-colored umbrellas. The aromas of coffee and tea danced with the music and swirled in the air. The cups and cutlery clinked, and friends chatted and laughed. Perhaps she and Aysha could go here sometime. She smiled broadly again. She couldn't wait to tell Aysha the news.

Near where they lived, she passed a pizza shop. She opened her pouch, looking at the few bills that remained. Eagerly, she entered, emerging several minutes later with a pile of boxes in her arms. She distributed the pizza to the homeless in her neighborhood, sharing the celebratory moment with them.

As Li was handing out another box to a group of men, one of them asked, "You the one who got the guys at the bank caught?" Li smiled and nodded. He hit her hand with the pizza away. "I don't want your pizza!" he yelled. "Robin's mad."

Li paused, unsure what he meant.

"If you don't want the pizza, I want it." Another homeless man came and took the box from her.

"SHAOLINA!" Li turned to see Aysha running down the street towards her. As she reached Li, she urgently tugged her hand. "Look! Look! I *have* to show you something, quick!"

She pulled Li to a nearby fast-food restaurant with a television inside. "Look!" She pointed up. "You're on the news!"

Li saw grainy footage of herself at the bank, striking the robbers. The screen then blinked to show a brunette reporter; a banner beneath her image read: "Homeless Turned Hero."

The screen then replayed the footage of Li. Aysha winced then hooted. "*Girl!* I'll be sure not to steal *your* things!"

Li turned to Aysha, smiling. "The bank has given me a job!"

Aysha gasped. "I'm so happy for you!"

"So how about we go and celebrate?" Li offered. "I want to take you to dinner at a Chinese restaurant."

Aysha laughed. It had been a long time since she'd eaten in a restaurant.

That evening, they made an effort to appear more presentable. They combed their hair and wore their best clothes. As they approached the restaurant, their eyes were met with a string of red Chinese lanterns glowing outside. Entering, they found milky walls decorated with red scrolls containing auspicious Chinese characters. Red paper dragons dangled from the ceiling. A vending machine hummed in the corner. On the grey ceramic floors stood a fish tank, its waters foggy. It contained a few live crab and fish, and plastic aquarium plants that swayed with the current. A ceiling fan circulated delicious aromas.

Aysha and Li seated themselves on wooden chairs at a corner table. They looked around, waiting for someone to serve them. No one seemed to be around, so Aysha quickly slipped the various sauce bottles from the table into her bag.

Li's eyes widened.

"*Shhhhhh!*" Aysha raised a finger to her lips. "Fast food can be bland. You need some spice and flavoring."

"We won't have to eat from the dumpsters anymore, remember?" Li said. "I got a job."

Aysha smiled, then said, "Old habits." The bottles stayed in her bag.

A waitress emerged through swinging doors and approached with menus. They studied the options, scanning the prices before looking at the dishes. The waitress came back a few minutes later. "Are you ready to order?"

Li nodded and pointed to the menu, "I'll take the vegetable noodle soup." The waitress scribbled down her order and turned to Aysha.

"And I'll have the chicken fried rice."

Once the waitress was gone, Aysha flashed a smile at Li. "This is my favorite Chinese dish. My mom used to make it for me."

Li returned an excited smile. She hadn't eaten Chinese food since leaving home.

Their eyes widened when their bowls were placed before them. Li held her chopsticks and tried the vegetables in her bowl. It wasn't exactly like the food from home, but it was closer than anything she'd had since arriving in America. As she kept eating, she tasted not the flavors but the emotions, as though she was eating not to fill her stomach but to feed her soul.

Once her bowl was nearly empty, Li sat back and looked around the place. A Chinese family in a corner caught her attention—parents with a little boy and girl. She could see the glimmer of joy in their eyes as they ate their food, shared stories, and laughed together.

Tears welled up. A warm hand touched hers. "I know you miss your family," Aysha said softly. "But one day, you'll see them again."

Li smiled at her, and sympathy flickered in her eyes. She knew the same was not true for Aysha. Not knowing what to say, she simply clasped Aysha's hand.

After Li had paid for their dinner, the waitress left them two fortune cookies.

"This is my favorite part!" Aysha squealed. Li had never seen a fortune cookie before. She watched curiously as Aysha broke it in two and pulled out a long white strip of paper. She read out her fortune, "*Great things come to those who believe in themselves. I guess there's no harm in that,*" she laughed. "What's yours?"

Li cracked open the cookie, then read her slip of paper: "*The winds of change will blow your way. Be careful what they'll blow away.*"

The reward money from the bank enabled Li to rent a small, furnished apartment in an old building, and she invited Aysha to live with her. The apartment had beige walls, worn hardwood floors, and basic furniture. But to Li and Aysha, it was palatial.

When Li first stepped into her bedroom, she put her backpack down on the floor, not quite believing she finally had a safe, stable place to rest her few belongings. Opening the apartment's cabinets and cupboards, she was taken aback by their spaciousness and wondered what she could fill them with. They seemed to offer her new space for a new life.

For the first time in months, she slept on a bed. She had forgotten the luxurious comfort of a mattress beneath her and the peace of mind that came with a stable shelter above her. Sometimes, in the middle of the night, she would hear the buzz of a police radio or a gunshot, and her heart would leap. But then she would lie her head back down, remembering that she was a safe distance from it all.

When she took her first shower, the warm water was like a pristine tropical waterfall, a luxury on her skin. It pushed the street dirt away from her body and down the drain. She felt deliciously clean. In many ways, this apartment heralded a clean start for her.

Instead of eating leftovers from the dumpster, she bought produce from the grocery store. She had a kitchen now, in which she would cook healthy meals for herself and Aysha. Giving her body nutritious food, she felt her energy levels rise.

Returning to her Shaolin training routine, she awoke before dawn and ran in the quiet parks and along trails, seeing only the trees, birds, and a few other early-morning joggers. She sprinted up and climbed down outdoor stairs, just as she had done at the temple. But now, she was panting. *I've gotten weaker,* she realized. *I need to improve.* She pushed herself. Sometimes, Aysha joined her on a run, and Li introduced her to some exercises and self-defense techniques.

The apartment was a new start for Aysha as well. She felt she no longer had an excuse for her drinking, which she had relied upon to emotionally escape her homelessness. So she joined support groups to curtail her addiction. With Li's encouragement, she also re-enrolled in high school. Sometimes, she felt hopelessly behind and was tempted to return to drinking to ease her stress. She had big arguments with Li during those times. But Li continued to encourage her, teaching her meditation and alternative ways to resolve her anxiety.

For the first time, now that she had a stable address, Li sent money to her family in China. The first remittance she sent back home filled her with a great sense of achievement. She also wrote them letters every month, sharing her experiences, and looked forward to the letters they wrote back. These letters were their only line of communication, as her family had neither a phone nor a computer.

CHAPTER 21

A few months later

"**BREAKING NEWS:** Another Bank Robbery Foiled

Two men are in custody after a bank security guard foiled a robbery in progress in Palo Alto, California on Wednesday.

The would-be robbers stole the security guard's weapons, then demanded cash and threatened to open fire on the tellers.

Despite having been disarmed, the security guard was able to neutralize the robbers. He credits his success to Shaolin techniques he learned as part of a new security guard training program, developed by Shaolin monk and training officer Shaolina.

This is yet another robbery foiled in California this year. Police are investigating whether there is a larger link between the many attempts.

The men are scheduled to appear in court on November 14."

"The California Times – Exclusive Interview with Shaolina

On Thursday, *The California Times* spoke with Shaolina, a Shaolin monk and training officer whose security guard training techniques have helped stop a series of robbery attempts this year. The following are excerpts from that interview.

CT: What is the secret behind your training program's success?

Shaolina: I teach the security guards efficient Shaolin techniques, like pressure points, deflection, and mental tricks. A guard of any age or size can use these. And since everyone has weak points, it works no matter how big the robber is. Also, security guards stand on their feet for hours at a time but must stay alert at all times. So our Shaolin training includes mental conditioning.

CT: You've helped stop yet another bank robbery. How does it feel to be a hero again?

Shaolina: I feel very proud of the security guards. They're the ones who deserve the credit. They work very hard.

CT: At twenty years old, you're a role model to many youths. What would you like to tell them?

Shaolina: I don't think I'm a role model. Like everyone, I have strengths and weaknesses. Youths should learn from as many people as possible, not just one."

Li was in her office at the bank, reading the newspapers with a smile on her face.

A knock sounded on her door. "Come in!" Li said.

It was the secretary. "A man named Josh is here to see you. He said he's from a film production company. Shall I let him in?"

"Yes, thank you," Li replied. She wondered what had brought him here.

A few seconds later, Josh walked through the doorway. "Hi, Shaolina! Remember me?"

Li rose from behind her desk. "Of course I do." She shook his hand.

Josh noticed that she looked different from when he had last seen her. Her hair, like black silk, now skimmed her shoulders. She wore a white collared shirt with the sleeves rolled back.

"Please, sit down, Josh." She motioned toward a chair.

He sat and immediately began. "Remember when you first came and asked for a job as a stunt double?"

She took a breath, then nodded.

"*Well*," Josh said excitedly, "we now have something better for you! Director Stevenson and I noticed you're popular among the young generation. *So…* we've decided to offer you a guest role on a teen TV series." He paused, waiting to see her reaction. Li showed no emotion. "It's about young undercover cops delving into youth crime," he continued, passing the letter of offer across her desk. It detailed the production, timeline, compensation, travel requirements, and other information.

Li glanced at the paper, then settled back in her office chair. Not too long ago, she wouldn't have thought twice about his offer. But now, she had a stable job with a good salary. It covered her rent and basic living expenses, leaving plenty to send back home. She looked at Josh, still in thought.

"We'll pay you well," he said, "and it's a good opportunity for you."

Li thought about her family. It wouldn't hurt to take another job if it would help her reach her goal and return home faster.

With that, she signed the contract.

Li's role lasted only a few episodes. Entering the series as a new cop from a neighboring town, she won over the audience with her cool and creative fighting skills.

In one scene, Li's fists were curled tightly around a briefcase of money. "You have five seconds to give me that briefcase," a thief said while pointing a gun at her.

Li gritted her teeth. Her gun lay beside the thief's foot—several meters away from her. *Was the money worth sacrificing her life?*

"Fine, take it!" she declared, then threw the briefcase upward. While he looked up to catch it, Li leaped in the air towards the briefcase, then spun and kicked it. It hit the thief in the face, knocking him out.

All of Li's scenes involved her defeating brawny, armed criminals using only her wits and martial arts. She did not have much dialogue, apart from yelling one-liners. But her body language spoke volumes about her. From the natural grace in her movements to the graciousness in her eyes, the audience fell in love with her. Episodes with her involved had by far the highest ratings.

In one of Li's scenes, she had to save the son of a billionaire who was being held captive in an enemy's mansion. Li entered the film studio to find Director Stevenson talking and gesturing to a tall actor. When Li's eyes landed on this man, she froze. Piercing green eyes dominated his face. They glimmered like emeralds and had flecks of golden in them. He had rosebud lips, a strong jaw line, and a light brown beard. His shoulders were broad and his muscles lean. Li's surroundings suddenly became dark. All she could see was the man. The background noise around her faded. All she could hear was the thudding of her heart. She was lost in his deep green eyes. She could feel her body become hot. Li had never felt like this before, and it both puzzled and slightly frightened her. The director walked away from the actor.

"Shaolina, get in position," Josh ordered. "Shaolina? Shaolina!"

Li was in her own world, gazing at the actor. "SHAOLINA!!!" Director Stevenson yelled through his megaphone, snapping her from her trance.

"Sorry! I'm here! I'm here!" She ran over and took her position.

"All right, stand next to Derek. ACTION!"

In the ensuing scene, Li helped free the man and bring him to safety. They ran down a hallway, only to see the enemy's henchmen charging towards them. Li neutralized them one after another. When she and the man reached the main gates of the mansion, Director Stevenson called, "CUT!"

Li looked up at Derek standing beside her, but he simply walked away without a glance. Watching him leave, Li wondered why she felt so forlorn.

During her final appearance, Li was standing in front of a gangster, her eyes wide with horror. The gangster had fired a shot at her friend, who was also a cop. It was too late to stop the bullet, so she jumped before her friend. The bullet hit her spine. She let out a cry of pain and fell to the ground.

That cry of pain was echoed by fans everywhere as they saw their favorite new character killed off. There was a storm on social media as fans lashed out at the studio for this "huge mistake." They wanted to see more of Shaolina, and some refused to believe that such a great character was really gone.

As Li had no social media accounts, she remained oblivious to the storm of her fans' indignation.

After the last episode was a wrap, everyone involved in "Undercover Youth" had a season finale celebration. The venue was a five-star Beverly Hills hotel. Li received two tickets to the party and yearned for Aysha to accompany her. But Aysha had final exams, leaving Li on her own.

For guidance, Li flipped through the pages of celebrity gossip magazines, studying the styles, dresses, and makeup of other celebrities. Staring at the lights, sparkle, and general glamor of the pictures, she felt a flutter of excitement. She couldn't wait until the party. But these dresses looked pricey. She withdrew $200 from her cash box, then thought: *Derek will be at the party.* She took another hundred dollars and went dress shopping.

After walking past a series of shops, she stopped in her tracks and gazed at a dress on display. It was made of deep-red silk that curved along the mannequin's body and had a sweetheart neckline. Li imagined herself wearing the dress with red lipstick and her hair twisted to fall over one shoulder. With that image in mind, she continued to the store entrance.

As she reached for the long, shiny steel bar that served as a door handle, a security guard clad in a black tuxedo opened the door for her.

Li stepped in and was met with a now-familiar blast of cold air. She could see white marble floors reflecting the golden lights that shone above them. A crystal chandelier dangled from the high ceiling. There were only a few racks, and they were widely spaced, each under its own spotlight. A few mannequins were posed throughout the store, wearing edgy runway clothes.

Li caught a glimpse of herself in a mirror along the wall. Shapeless faded jeans and a striped shirt hung on her body. She was suddenly conscious of their inferior quality. She averted her eyes from her reflection and focused on the red dress.

High heels clicked on the marble floor. A brunette woman in a white dress approached her. "Can I help you?"

"I'd like to see that red dress, please." Li walked over to the mannequin.

The woman crossed her arms and followed as Li reached for the thick tag that hung from the dress. She saw "$12" followed by some zeroes that her brain could not register. "How much is this?" She turned to the woman.

"Twelve thousand," the woman spoke through her nose.

After the word "thousand," all Li heard was a tuning fork sound ringing in her ears. Everything became dark, with only the light of the exit sign visible. She headed out the door while her head spun, trying to grasp how a dress could be worth so much.

As she still needed something to wear, she went to a prom shop near her apartment. This place was the opposite of the boutique store: gray carpeted floor, low ceiling, and white fluorescent lighting. The entire store was a maze of racks, each stuffed with dresses, from puffy ball gowns to body-hugging sheaths replete with colorful sequins. Sorting through them, Li realized they were still above her budget. Now she started looking not at the dresses themselves but at their price tags, moving from tag to tag.

Finally, she found herself at the end of the store, at a sale rack. She reached for a black satin A-line dress, then looked around for a salesclerk, to ask if she could try it on. But the store seemed empty. So she slipped into a changing room and put it on. Then she stepped before the mirror outside.

The flashy shine of satin couldn't compare to the sophisticated luminescence of silk. But this dress was at least affordable. She felt comfort in its blackness, just as the gloomy find comfort in clouds.

She almost jumped out of the dress as a voice sounded from behind her.

"Why so dark?"

Li turned around to see a short woman in her early fifties, with a round face, large hips, casual clothes, and comfy flat shoes.

"You're young! You should wear something bright for your prom!" Li smiled uneasily. "You have a beautiful slim figure. You should show it off! Stay there, I have something for you." The woman tromped towards a rack against the wall and pulled out a light-orange mermaid gown. "Try this," she said.

The color reminded Li of her orange robes at the Shaolin Temple. Immediately, it lifted her spirits. She stepped into it and stood before the mirror, turning to see herself from different angles. The dress hugged her lithe frame and showed off her curves.

"*Ahh*, you like this one," the woman said.

Li did. The bold color gave her confidence. Then she saw the price tag hanging on the side.

The shop assistant noticed Li's expression fall. "Don't worry," she said, "I can give it to you for the same price as that black one."

Li gasped, grateful, and glad to have found the right dress at the right price.

CHAPTER 22

The day of the celebration arrived. With a blend of excitement and nervousness mingling in her stomach, Li dressed in her orange gown and took a cab to the venue.

The police had blocked off the road in front of the hotel, so the cab stopped a block away and Li walked the rest of the distance.

The venue was pulsing with sound and movement, and as she approached it, Li felt her own pulse accelerate. Beams of bright lights were shooting up to the dark sky and crisscrossing. Along the sidewalk was a line of glistening black limousines. One after another, they stopped at the entrance to drop off their stars. Guards clad in black tuxedos opened their doors. And out stepped glamorous women dressed in gowns similar to those Li had seen at the expensive boutique. They all had dates, whose arms they held as they walked down the red carpet, smiling and waving to the cameras.

Li clasped her arm. With each step closer, she felt more nervousness than excitement churning in her stomach.

Along the red carpet was a large white board with the printed logos of sponsors. In front of it, movie stars posed for a barrage of camera flashes, showing off different angles of their bodies and flashing their perfect white smiles. Li was struck by the sparkling jewelry embracing their necks and the dazzling diamonds dripping from their ears. The celebrities smiled and struck poses like they were the most satisfied and accomplished people in the world.

Seeing them, Li felt out of place. Her orange gown now seemed costumey, and under the bright lights, her tastefully made-up face felt suddenly bare. She couldn't bring herself to step before the white boards and pose like the other celebrities. She didn't even know how to pose; she lacked that surge of confidence that would buoy her up, lift her chin, or guide her hand naturally to her hip. So instead, she kept behind the stanchions like the rest of the guests.

Some people called her name: "Shaolina! Shaolina!" But under the flashing lights, the crowd was an amorphous blob to Li. She didn't know where the voices were coming from or where to look, so she gave a quick smile and waved her hands to no one in particular. Then she slipped inside the hotel.

As she approached the ballroom entrance, Li heard waves of loud jazz music, along with laughter, chatter, and the clink of glasses, spilling out from the doors. She took a deep, steadying breath and entered.

Inside, a succession of large, crystal chandeliers dimly suffused the room with gold. Throughout the room sprawled round dinner tables packed with elegant guests. Walking across the cushiony dark green carpet, Li found her name on a seating card at a table in the corner.

She slid into her seat with a smile and glanced around at her table companions. Everyone seemed engrossed in their own conversations. Li turned to the woman beside her—mid-thirties, brunette, navy blue dress.

"Hi, my name is Shaolina."

"Hi!" the woman said quickly, then returned to talking to her friend.

Li compressed her lips. She turned to the man on her right—late twenties, tall, lean, dark hair, brown eyes, white suit. "Hi, I'm Shaolina," she said.

He gave her a dry smile, then turned back to his friend. He must have made a face because his friend was silent for a second, then let out a chortle before they resumed their conversation.

Li was slightly hurt. She turned her attention to the guests at surrounding tables. They were laughing and chatting. Everyone here already knew each other; she felt there was no room for her.

"Wine?" a waiter approached her with a bottle.

"No, water is fine," Li responded, as she did not drink alcohol. The man beside her stole a quick, judgmental glance at her. As the waiter left, Li cradled her glass while looking around tentatively. She urged herself to smile, to appear confident if any eyes were to look her way. Suddenly, all the music faded.

Ting. Ting. Ting.

Director Stevenson appeared on stage, tapping a spoon against his glass to claim the guests' attention. To Li's relief, all the chatter ceased as everyone turned their heads to him.

"Refreshing, huh, to see me yell at you using a microphone rather than my usual megaphone," the director began. The guests laughed. "But in all seriousness, this night is to…" And the director made a speech thanking the entire film cast and crew for making the show a success. Then he said, "Here's a toast to the end of one successful season and the beginning of many more to come." He raised his glass in the air.

All the guests raised their glasses. "*Cheers!*" they said in unison. Li's voice was small.

"Now, let's enjoy ourselves tonight!" he yelled into the microphone. The music resumed and so did the conversation and laughter. Wait staff weaved around the tables, taking orders and serving dishes.

Li looked down at the menu and realized she had no idea what the dish names meant. She glanced at the other people at her table to see whether they understood.

"*Ooooh!*" the woman beside her sat up in delight. "They're serving *Hachis parmentier!*"

"My favorite!" her friend added.

The dish names were just pretentions, Li knew. But they sent a loud message to her that was inaudible to the upper-class guests: *You don't belong here.*

She was trying to decipher the menu when a waiter appeared from behind her. "What would you like to order?" he asked.

"I, uh—" Her mind scrabbled for a response that wouldn't embarrass her. "I'll take this one." She pointed randomly to the middle of the menu.

"The pan-seared *foie gras*?"

"Ye–yes."

As the waiter came with her dish, she saw a plump piece of meat on her plate. Too embarrassed to reveal that she didn't understand the menu and wanted to change her order, she picked up her fork and poked at the few vegetables around the meat.

She regretted her wastefulness. Keeping her gaze on her plate, she found herself having to swallow her food around a knot in her throat.

Maybe I should walk around. She got up from the table so she could breathe. *I wonder where Derek is.* Instantly, her heart felt lighter. She wondered what he looked like outside the film studio. She craned her neck as she roamed around, but could not see Derek anywhere.

The party was finally over, and Li was glad to scurry out of the ballroom. While the other stars got into their limousines, Li walked along the sidewalk, looking for a cab. A drop fell on her hair. Looking up, she saw gray clouds gathering. *I'd better get home quickly.* Caught up in her thoughts, something inside urged her frantically to turn around. She did, and her eyes flew wide with surprise.

Derek! He was dressed in an immaculate black tuxedo. His hair was combed back, and his face was dashing. He was walking along the sidewalk. As he headed towards her, Li felt butterflies in her stomach, their wings seeming to lift her off to flight.

He had one arm reaching behind him. That's when Li noticed he was holding a woman's hand. Mellifluous laughter rippled towards Li. She shattered into pieces, and all the butterflies in her stomach died.

The woman came into full view. She was tall and slim, and wearing a long, silver dress replete with crystals. A toned, tanned leg peeked from the slit at the side of her dress. She had full breasts, and diamonds dangled from her ears. Curly blond hair framed her high cheeks. She had sparkling blue eyes and a perfect white smile that mesmerized Li.

Li stepped to the side as they walked past without even acknowledging her. With a hand on the small of his date's back, Derek led her to their limousine, which waited at the corner of the street. Li remained fixed in place, watching as they drove away. She thought about the woman. She was a bounty of curves while Li was a bundle of nerves, and she was effortlessly charming while Li was helplessly boring. Li looked down at her flat chest and her square body, and thought about her ethnic face. Who was she to think Derek would ever even look at her?

The gray clouds above rumbled, then broke into torrents of rain. Her hair and dress became drenched, but she didn't care, because right there, all she could feel was the agonizing aching in her heart. It wasn't just Derek. She reflected on the night's events—the alienating language of the menu, the haughty guests, and the cold shoulders they'd given her. No matter what she did, she would never fit in. She would always be the wrong gender, the wrong race, the wrong class. They did not connect with her as though she was a human like them. No, she sensed an isolating barrier between her and everyone else. It was as if every time they stared into her eyes, they saw the slant rather than the soul behind. Every time they looked at her porcelain face, they saw a china doll rather than a real person. There was a shell encasing her, and she yearned to break it. Break it and tell people that inside, she was just like them.

Pant, pant, pant.

Someone was breathing heavily, drawing Li out of her internal tirade. She turned around to the source of the sound. It was a short, bald man with a big belly, who appeared to be in his early sixties. He was running from the thrashing sheet of rain towards his limousine across the street, and he stepped into a puddle on the sidewalk, then slipped.

Terror filled his heart as he felt his body fall backwards, at the mercy of gravity. He tightened his eyes and braced himself.

But what he felt next was not the pavement but a pair of hands, holding him up. Opening his eyes, he saw Li's face. With a lightning-quick reaction, she had caught him before he hit the ground.

Rrrrrip.

Li glanced down at her tight mermaid gown and saw a tear along the side of her leg. She didn't care. She steadied the heavy man to his feet. The man, who had unconsciously been holding his breath, exhaled. "Oh thank you! Thank you!" He looked over at his savior—soaked in rain, with a torn gown. "Do you have a ride home?" he asked.

"I'm waiting for a cab."

"Please, join me in my limousine. I'll give you a ride." The two scurried across the street towards his waiting limousine. As Li ducked her head to get inside, her mouth gaped at the posh interior. She settled herself on a long, dry, black leather seat, then gazed at the twinkling lights on the roof and the mini bar at the side. *I can't wait to tell Aysha about this!* she thought.

"If I'm not mistaken…" The man's voice, once the car was moving, drew her attention back to him. "Aren't you Shaolina?"

"Yes, I am." Li was surprised he recognized her.

"So *you're* the latest sensation on 'Undercover Youth'! I've been thinking about you for a while. I've seen you act and perform martial arts. Your fighting skills are very impressive!"

"Thank you," Li replied.

"I've yet to introduce myself. I'm David Seagull, a movie director. Can you come by my office next week?" He gave her his address.

Li smiled to herself, anticipating another role as a guest actress.

CHAPTER 23

When next week came, Li saw Director Seagull in his office.

He told her he was directing a new action film called *Cop Family*. It was about a Chinese cop named Brad Lee who marries Jennifer, an American cop, and the two have a beautiful daughter named Amy. Brad Lee, who is a Kung Fu master, trains Amy in the art, and when Amy turns twenty-three, she becomes a skilled cop. But she falls in love with a criminal she's after, and because the criminal, Travis, loves her too, he turns himself in. After serving his prison time, he ends up working as a cop himself, using his knowledge of criminal mentalities to catch other crooks. Travis asks for Amy's hand in marriage. It turns out that the story is history repeating itself, as it's the same way Brad Lee had met his own wife.

Director Seagull saw many similarities between Li and the character Amy, so he offered Li the role. She was euphoric. This was a big movie with a big budget, famous co-stars, a wide mainstream audience, and excellent publicity. It would elevate her to the next level and open doors for even greater opportunities and higher pay.

Once Li signed the film contract, her life was a whirlwind of transformation. As her acting role paid a six-figure salary and took all of her time and focus, she resigned from her job at the bank. Meanwhile, Aysha flew to the East Coast to begin college, where she had decided to pursue her passion, literature. Li funded her college education.

Since arriving in America, Li had thirsted for knowledge about how to be more like a woman. In her character, Amy, she found her personal guide. Li followed a new diet and exercise regime to develop Amy's body. Standing before the mirror, she saw herself becoming curvier. She caught her reflection at different angles, loving the way her fuller hips made her waist appear thinner.

Her character had a beauty team on set. Li drank in whatever makeup and hairstyles they put on her, taking mental notes for her personal use. She also took note of their wardrobe choices for Amy. Then she sought to find similar clothes for herself: padded bras to amplify her breasts, a crop top that revealed her abs, and skinny jeans that flaunted her toned legs. For the first time, when she walked on the streets, she turned heads and caught admiring glances. There was a confidence in her stride, as she finally felt like a woman. The sidewalk became her runway, the sun her stage lighting, and the shop windows her mirrors.

In her small apartment, Li would pace, script in hand. At first she would walk—walk around in Amy's shoes and let Amy walk around in her mind. But then the empty seat at the dining table would catch her eye, and she would pause. She looked at the empty places Aysha used to occupy, looked at the empty rooms where she used to study, listened to the empty silence her voice used to fill. And in those moments, the emptiness would seep into her.

So when she was on the couch alone, Li would pretend that Amy was sitting beside her. To explore her character, she'd ask her questions: *What hobbies do you enjoy? How would you describe your default demeanor? What do you think of other people?* She fleshed out Amy's mind, movements, and mannerisms until Amy became more dimensional. Then she memorized and internalized her lines until she felt the border between her and Amy blur.

When the director called, "Action!" she was no longer sure whether she breathed life into her character or her character breathed life into her. They had become one. She was disconnected from her body, suspended in space, only a spirit—nameless, transcending categories and parts. There was no ego, there was no self, and yet she felt more herself than ever before. She was flowing along a river, carried, carried away.

Then the director called, "Cut!" and the river ahead abruptly vanished, leaving her to drop onto hard ground. Cast and crew complimented her. "You crushed it!" "That performance will get the people at the Academy talking." But when a crewmember asked her how she acted so naturally, she could not answer. It was like she had simultaneously tuned in and zoned out. After the first screening, whispers spread that this would be big. The winds of fame would blow their way. Eagerly, the cast embraced each other and braced themselves.

Then the movie was released on the big screens. It received critical acclaim. Fans and film critics alike admired the plot twists and the technical qualities. Many also liked the authenticity of Li's performance. They admired the fighter in Amy's spirit and the lover in her soul. The way her character moved through Li and moved her had moved audiences as well.

To publicize the film, Li had to go on a promotional tour. For the first time, she traveled the globe and entered the world of private jets and five-star hotels. For the first time, she experimented with and explored different food, fine wines—she'd given up being teetotal—fancy restaurants, and posh clubs. She began to buy herself designer clothes and jewelry.

Standing on the red carpet amidst a sea of camera flashes and fans' faces, Li felt her limbs liquefy. She could melt in such moments. She had never imagined that thousands of people she had never met could love her so much. Celebrities who had never talked to her now wanted to befriend her. Surrounded by spotlights and screams, she felt that she was spinning and spinning in glee, until she wasn't sure whether she was spinning or the world was spinning around her egocentric self.

The film brought Li a fortune. With the money she sent home, her family was able to buy back their family land rights. Li felt relief and elation at this momentous achievement, but the momentum of her success propelled her onward, leaving her little time to think and absorb it all.

She signed a contract for a new film, an action-drama called *Black Mountain*. She also gained a contract with a sportswear company to model their clothes, footwear, and moisture-resistant makeup. With her earnings, Li moved out of her shoddy neighborhood and purchased an upscale house in Hollywood Hills.

She also appeared on several talk shows. On one of these occasions, Li was backstage at a late-night talk show, pacing her breathing and mentally running through some of her prepared answers. Across the studio, sitting behind a large wooden desk, was the host: a woman in her mid-fifties with a red bob, black-rimmed glasses, and an edgy white blazer. The photographic backdrop was of Los Angeles at night.

With a husky voice, the host began, "Our next guest tonight is a star who's been through quite a journey. From homeless on the streets to a civic hero to an actress in the blockbuster film of the year, *Cop Family*, she has stolen the hearts of millions around the world... Please welcome—Shaolina!"

The audience broke into wild applause as Li strode on stage, waving and smiling. She was wearing high heels, skinny white pants, a sleeveless black halter top, and solitaire earrings. Her hair was up in a bun. She perched on the edge of the guest couch, her back very straight. The audience continued to cheer, still on their feet. "Shaolina!" "Shaolina, we love you!"

The calls went on. Li laughed and stood up again. She clasped her hands and bowed her head. "Thank you." Then she sat back down.

"Wow." The host shook her head and turned to Li. "First of all, congratulations on your phenomenal success."

"Thank you."

"How does it feel?"

"It feels like I'm living in a dream," Li said. "I still can't believe it."

"I don't blame you. It all happened so quickly," the host said. "Your story inspires millions of young people. What would you say to those who still don't believe they can make it?"

Li turned to face audience. "I want to tell you ... if you're driven, where you come from won't hold you back from where you can go. Who you start out as won't define who you can be. A person can move from the streets to Wall Street, a poor farmer can grow into a wealthy businesswoman, and illiterate parents can raise highly educated children. People like me, from different backgrounds and with different stories, are connected by a single storyline—the American dream."

The audience broke into applause and cheers.

"You've helped prevent many bank robberies," the host said. "I've heard that you continue to do that. How do you find the time?"

Li was confused. "Actually, I resigned from the bank to focus entirely on acting."

The host was still not convinced. She felt that Li was hiding something. With narrowed eyes, as though trying to see the person deep in her soul, she asked, "Who are you really, Shaolina?"

"I'm just a lucky person," Li said matter-of-factly.

"I think you're more than that," she said. "Ladies and gentlemen, Shaolina!"

The audience cheered.

CHAPTER 24

The climax of this whirlwind of changes was an Oscar nomination for Best Supporting Actress. To share this momentous event, Li bought first-class flight tickets for her mother and Mei, inviting them to visit her for the Oscars ceremony.

On the day of their arrival, Li felt a mixture of excitement and nervousness as she waited in the airport's arrivals area. She was carrying a large bouquet of flowers. It had been over three years since Li had seen them. She had always been a son in her mother's eyes. She wondered how her mother would react now to seeing her as a woman.

"Shaolina, Shaolina!" someone's voice called. Li turned to see a young man with long hair and a large video camera mounted on his shoulder. He held out a microphone to her with his other hand. "Who's the bouquet for?"

Li smiled. "My mother," she replied. She returned her gaze to the arrivals gate.

"Are they coming for the Oscars?"

"Yes."

"I must say, you look great! You've changed a lot since before you started filming *Cop Family*. What's your secret?"

"It's all about diet and exercise."

"So what do you think about—"

Li suddenly spotted her mother and Mei walking out the gate, pulling suitcases on wheels. They looked exactly the same as Li remembered.

"*Bye!*" she dismissed the reporter as she rushed forward to her family, an excited smile spread across her face. She waved.

Mei looked around the reception hall, not seeming to find Li anywhere.

"She said she would be here." She turned to her mother. "Mom! Mei!"

They turned to see a woman waving in their direction and walking over to them in high heels. She had long, light-brown hair and wore a silky white blouse with the front tucked into skinny black jeans. Over her shoulder was a small handbag, its strap of interwoven silver metal and black leather hanging elegantly.

"Is that?" Mei strained her eyes as the woman approached. "Mom! That's Shaolina!" Mei's spirits jumped as her jaw dropped.

They ran towards her, and all three embraced tightly.

"Wow, you've changed a lot," Mei said. "You look different even from the pictures you've sent us." She swallowed, still absorbing the fact that this was her sister.

Lian was quiet, looking at her daughter. Li looked into her mother's eyes, searching for an answer. Lian smiled.

"You look beautiful," she finally said. Li smiled back, her lips quivering with emotion, feeling her mother's acceptance.

As they were walking out, a teenage girl squealed and ran towards Li. "Shaolina! Shaolina! I'm a big fan. Can I please get a selfie with you?"

Li posed with the girl as she took the shot with her phone. She shrieked in delight. "Can I hug you?" Li gave her an embrace. "O.M.G. I can't wait to tell my friends! They'll be so jealous!" She laughed and ran off.

Mei and Lian looked from each other to Li and back again, feeling pride buoy in their chest.

As they exited the airport, Mei spotted some cabs. "There's a taxi here!" she cried.

"No need," Li replied. "We're driving home."

"You didn't tell us that you drive," Lian said, surprised.

"This is Los Angeles. Everyone does."

Li led them to the parking lot. There, Mei's eyes lit on the smallest car— a milky-white Mini. "Is this it?" She headed towards it.

Li pressed a button on her fob, but the headlights of the Mini did not flash. Instead, it summoned to life a sleek, dark-blue Mercedes convertible.

"Wooow!" Mei's eyes widened as she approached it. "*This* is your car?" She gazed at her reflection in its gleaming body. Li smiled, enjoying her sister's awe. "It looks so expensive!"

Li opened the door for her mother to sit in the front while Mei hopped in the back, feeling the seat's soft yet firm cream-colored leather.

Li lowered the convertible top, then drove out of the parking lot.

Mei couldn't stop gaping. She felt the air rushing against her face as a series of streetlamps seemed to fly past. "Wheeeeeeeeeee!" Mei screamed.

Lian was grasping onto to the sides of her seat. "Shaolina! Don't drive so fast!" she yelled. "We're not in a rush. And Mei, stop screaming! People will think you're crazy!"

Luckily for Lian, the streets in front of them were soon congested, and Li was forced to slow down. To a halt. They were stuck in traffic. Li looked up ahead on the right. "Look at that billboard," she said. Lian and Mei turned to see a woman in a sports bra, leggings, and running shoes advertising for a sportswear company.

"Yeah, so what?" Mei said.

"Look at her face," Li offered.

They did. Then they gasped. "Shaolina, that's you!" Mei couldn't believe it. Lian looked at the billboard photo, beaming with pride, though also cringing slightly at how exposed her daughter's body was.

Once they got through traffic, Li began the ascent of Hollywood Hills.

"You've decided to live near a mountain again," remarked Mei. Li laughed, remembering the Shaolin Temple at the foot of Song Mountain.

They drove past a series of large mansions, concealed by tall fences and enshrouded by bushes, until they stopped before black iron gates. Seeing her, a guard in a sentry box pressed a button, opening the gates for them.

"Welcome to our home," Li said as she drove through the gates. Mei and her mother gazed out at a luscious carpet of bright green grass, orange and evergreen trees lining a stone pathway, and a large fountain in front of the house. As they stepped out of the car, their jaws dropped. Li's was an ultra-modern house—a two-story block made of glass and stone.

Stepping inside onto white marble floors washed in golden lights, they gazed up at the grand ceiling. Then they looked at the crisp white furniture and walls. A housekeeper approached and took their luggage.

Li turned to her family's awestruck faces. "I have a lot to show and tell you. But you must be tired. So I'll let you rest until dinner is ready," she said, and she led them to the guest rooms.

It was dark when Mei and her mother awoke. Mei walked on the cold marble floor towards the window. She could see tiny orange lights sparkling from the city below, like stars on the ground. This was not a dream. They actually were on a different side of the world, and this actually was Li's house.

They descended the stairs to find Li in the living room, the light of a large, muted television flickering on her.

"You're awake!" Li greeted. "Let's have dinner."

Mei's face brightened. "Awesome! I'm starving!" She descended the remaining staircase with a jovial bounce to her steps. Lian followed, more slowly.

Li led them to her dining hall, which had tall, frameless windows. It revealed a black night sky and yellow lamplight in the garden outside. The glass dining table was long enough to seat twelve guests. Li seated her mother at the head of the table while she and Mei sat to either side. Li's chef approached with their dishes.

"Thank you," Mei said to him in English as he put her plate before her. She looked at the white rectangular plate, which carried three sauce-painted orange circles. On the first circle was an oyster, on the second was a butterfly-cut jumbo shrimp, and on the third lay a deep-fried cube of sea bass.

Mei gobbled down all three. "I don't know what that was," she said as she slid her finger across the sauce on the plate. "But it was delicious." She licked her finger. "I'm still hungry though."

Li laughed. "Don't worry, there's more on the way."

The chef arrived with a huge pot of seafood: salmon as well as lobster and other shellfish. He served each of them a scoop, along with steamed rice and vegetables. Then he stood in the corner, one hand clasping the other.

Lian raised a spoon to her mouth, but then her eye caught the chef watching them. She lowered her spoon.

"Shaolina," she whispered, "tell this man to go away. We can serve ourselves. I don't feel comfortable with him constantly watching us."

Li asked the chef to leave, and he did.

Feeling more comfortable, Mei opened shellfish and popped their meat into her mouth. She glanced over at Li. "I had no idea you quit being a vegetarian," she said. But she did not care much for an explanation, happy simply that her sister could enjoy this seafood feast with her.

Finally came dessert: chocolate mousse with fresh berries. Mei felt herself melt. "This is the most delicious food I've ever had in my life!"

The women sat on patio chairs while looking out at the garden, cloaked in the night. Li poured tea into their cups. "So how are the villagers?" she asked.

"We no longer have to hide your identity," Lian said. "They heard about how you've become rich and famous. They say no wonder you became a successful actress—you managed to fool them all those years into thinking you were a boy. You were born to be an actress."

Bursting with excitement, Mei interjected, "And now they're saying that one girl like Shaolina is worth a thousand village boys!"

"Wow." Li put her teacup down. But in truth, she was surprised not by the villagers' transformed views but by the fact that she didn't care at all.

"Had I heard this three years ago," she said, "I would have been very proud and fulfilled. But now, I honestly don't care about their opinions. They're just a bunch of lowly villagers." She said this last part with a dash of resentment. Mei and her mother exchanged uncertain glances. "How about Uncle?" Li asked.

"No one wants to be in your uncle's shoes these days," Lian replied. "He didn't have much experience in the supermarket business, so he was an easy target. The city people cheated him, and he lost all his money. Before that, he gave his son a lot of money so he could be the big man. But that attracted the wrong crowd. His 'friends' led him into drugs and alcohol and used him. He became a drug addict. Your uncle couldn't bear the reality of losing his son and all his money. He had a stroke that has left him half-paralyzed. So they returned to the village with nothing but their house. But his son struggled in the village because he couldn't feed his addiction. He ran off to the city. No one's heard of him since."

"He deserves that," Li said. "He made our father's life and our lives miserable. His heart is like black charcoal. He deserves to burn."

Lian's and Mei's jaws dropped. They hadn't expected Li to be this bitter and vengeful.

Li rose up with a sudden fire in her eyes and paced over to the edge of the patio, turning her back to them. She lifted her chin, looking out into the distance. She recalled her uncle's mockery of her when she was at his house. The sound of the villagers' laughter washed over her again.

There was silence between them.

"Now, I want you to build for yourself the biggest house in the village," she finally said. "Bigger than Uncle's. Invite all the villagers for a feast. These people are low-minded and hungry. Give them some food so they can smile for you, respect you." She said this with a tone so bitter that it alarmed Lian and Mei. They began to worry about her, about losing their Li.

Lian spoke to her softly. "Now that we've bought back the family land and we have more than enough money, you can return to China. You don't have to stay here anymore."

Li's ferocious eyes pounced on her mother as she whirled around. "I don't blame you, *Mother*, you're used to sitting in dirt and poverty. But I'm not crazy enough to leave this opportunity here so I can go and do nothing with you in nowhere! So long as the money's coming, I won't turn it down. I'd be an idiot to let go of this life."

Her mother's worry now turned to fear. The air around them felt toxic, and Mei could barely breathe. Trying to change the ambience, Mei reminded her about those she had loved in her childhood. "A few days ago," she started, "I was in the marketplace and I saw monk Kai!" She put on a cheery smile. "He said your shifu and the monks always ask about you."

Li paced back to her chair and slumped down. "I pity them," she said, sliding her finger along the rim of her cup. "They're deceiving themselves, living in another world. We were so stupid. Enjoying the moon, the air, free things while lying to ourselves that we were content. But now I see that's just what the poor say to placate themselves in their poverty. Now I see that *this* is the real world," she looked around her, "the tangible, material world. If you have no money," her eyes darted back and forth between her mother and Mei, "you receive no respect. Look at what happened to us when we were poor; we were the laughingstocks of the village."

As she was talking, she noticed the expressions on their faces, and she broke off. She had said too much. It had been a long time since she'd had someone to vent to, someone with the context to understand her. But now, she could see she had stoked fear in their hearts. She waved her hands and tried to put on a bright smile. "Let's forget about all this," she said, "and just enjoy our time together."

Mei took a deep breath and leaned forward, speaking softly. "I want to share with you—"

But her mother lightly kicked her leg, under the table. When Mei looked to her, Lian gave her a slight shake of the head. Li did not notice the exchange.

"I'll let you rest now," Li said. "We have a lot of shopping to do tomorrow to prepare for the Oscars."

CHAPTER 25

The next day, Li took her mother and Mei to a posh boutique store. As soon as they stepped in, they felt out of place. But seeing the confident way Li moved ahead of them, and the way the store staff seemed to already know her, alleviated their discomfort. Soon after their arrival, a blond, middle-aged woman entered the store.

"Hi, Elizabeth!" Li beamed. She turned to her mother and Mei. "This is Elizabeth. She designs wardrobes for celebrities. I've hired her to pick out your dresses for the Oscars."

Mei and her mother smiled uneasily, seeing Elizabeth as a superfluous expenditure. They could pick out their own dresses.

"Elizabeth, this is my mother and my sister. They don't speak much English."

"No problem." Elizabeth shook their hands. Then she took a step back, analyzing Mei's body shape and skin tone. "I think I know just the right dress style for you."

She took Mei by the hand and led her into the fitting room area. Then she perused through the racks and pulled out an A-line dress made of peach silk chiffon. "Try this on." She handed it to Mei.

As Mei was getting into the dress, Li and her mother sat on a black velvet sofa, waiting. Lian hoped that Elizabeth was worth the extra cost. Mei stepped out of the fitting room with pressed lips. Upon seeing the dress, Lian mirrored her expression. The dress had no lace, no sparkle, no embroidery, nothing to wow her. But Li trusted Elizabeth.

"This is a silk chiffon Valentino dress," Elizabeth began. "The color is young and fresh. And a touch of sparkle will complete the youthful picture."

Li stood up and examined her sister in the dress. "I like the color on you. It brightens your face."

Mei glanced at the price tag hanging on the side of her dress. "How much does it say?"

Li checked for her. "It's $7,000," she said matter-of-factly.

Suddenly, the light chiffon felt heavy on her body. All she wanted to do was get out of it.

"Are you crazy?!" she snapped at Li. "With that money, we could clothe the entire village! Plus, I don't like it. It's plain. There's nothing on it. So why is it so expensive?"

"It doesn't matter whether you like it or not," Li responded. "What matters is what people at the Oscars will like. And Elizabeth knows their tastes."

Mei was not convinced. If the dress were red or white, at least she could stitch on some embroidery and wear it again for her wedding, maybe justify to herself the extravagant cost. But she would never wear this dress again. It was a waste of money.

She saw how important this was to her sister and her career, though, and she didn't want to embarrass her. Maybe they knew things she didn't. So she obliged.

Next came their mother's turn, at another store, where Elizabeth dressed Lian in black satin. "This is a classic Chanel dress. With pearl jewelry, it's perfect for her age," she said to Li.

"The black depresses me," Lian murmured. "But if it makes you happy, I can wear it."

On the day of the Oscars, Li's house was buzzing with makeup artists, hair stylists, and dressers, all prepping Li and her family for the big event. Then their limousine arrived. Glammed up and ready to go, Li and her family got inside.

During the ride, Li inundated them with advice. "Millions of people will be watching you. So you need to act perfectly. Always smile, no matter what you feel inside. If someone offers you something, say, 'Thank you.'" As she continued overloading them, Mei slumped in her seat. "Mei!" Li barked. "Keep your posture straight. Always. Your body language says a lot about you. And don't talk too much."

She kept going until the limousine came to a stop. They had arrived. Li immediately turned away from her family to face the window, heart pounding. This was her biggest red carpet event yet. Previously, she had stood on the sidelines, watching stars be handed out of their limousines for the Oscars. Now it was her turn.

The limousine driver, clad in an immaculate tuxedo, opened the door and held out his hand for her. As she stepped out, her golden ball gown billowed around her. The popping camera flashes lit up her face and the metallic fabric, making her feel like the dazzling sun. As her high heels touched the red carpet, an intense happiness caught her unexpectedly.

She closed her eyes, absorbing the moment. The roaring crowd. The lights. The attention and admiration. Her whole life had been a journey leading up to this moment. Opening her eyes, she walked forward, smiling, waving.

Ah! Mother and Mei! In the exuberance of the moment, she had forgotten about them. She looked behind to check on them. Her sister was smiling as she had been told. She looked cute in her peach dress. And her mother looked like a classy, powerful woman.

Li sighed in relief. Everything was going perfectly. All the money she had spent on them was well worth it.

She advanced and posed for the cameras. Hand on hip, she lifted her head. Then she gave the cameras a side view of her body. In her golden gown, she thought, *I am the sun, warming up fans and burning down foes.*

"Shaolina! Over here!" a cameraman called for Li to look in his direction.

"Shaolina! We love you!" fans cried.

Li thought of the whole world watching her from the sidelines while she shone on center stage. She looked over at the other celebrities. Now, she was one of them—the rich, famous, powerful elite.

As she continued walking and waving, the diamonds

on her hand sparkled with her. She wished the red carpet would stretch infinitely, that this moment would never end.

She passed a series of raised platforms, each hosting reporters from different TV networks. "Shaolina," called out a brunette in a maroon mermaid gown with a plunging neckline. Li stepped onto the platform while her mother and sister stayed a few steps behind her. "Congratulations, Shaolina, on your nomination for Best Supporting Actress."

"Thank you."

"This is your first ever nomination. How do you feel?"

"To be honest, I'm slightly nervous. I don't know what to expect."

The reporter laughed. "I have to say, you look stunning today! What are you wearing?"

"My gown is by Christian Dior, and these diamond earrings and bracelets are from Cartier."

"Absolutely stunning! Not just beautiful, but bright. We understand you're still helping to fight crime."

"I don't know what you're talking about."

The reporter laughed. "Ah! There's our modest monk!" she said to the camera, gesturing at the antithesis of a Shaolin monk.

But Li did not echo her laughter. The second occurrence of this remark made her uneasy.

"So who's with you today?" the reporter asked.

Li turned to her family behind her. "That's my mother and my sister."

"Hi Mom! Hi Sis!" The reporter waved to them.

They waved and smiled back, having their two seconds of fame on television.

"Great talking to you Shaolina!" The reporter touched her on the elbow. "Good luck tonight."

"Thank you." Li nodded at her, then waved to the cameras and descended the steps with her family.

After a few more brief interviews, Li and her family entered the grand Dolby Theatre, where Lian and Mei were guided to seats in the back balcony. Li walked to the second row on the main floor, where she greeted the other cast and crew. Their film had received numerous nominations.

Soon a performer entered the theatre from the back, singing as he descended the stairs, getting row after row of people on their feet as he passed them. By the time he reached the stage, all the guests were on their feet, swaying side to side and clapping with the beat. Li felt the waves of music rise in her chest and carry her soul. She looked around at the bright golden lights along the theatre, the high-class stars with their tuxedos and extravagant gowns. She was among them, dancing, clapping, and anticipating an Oscar.

When the performance finished, the crowd cheered and sat back down. The host emerged, and the Oscars got under way.

"Here are the nominees for Best Performance by an Actress in a Supporting Role."

Li's heart sprang as she heard her category being called. The screens now showed a clip of each nominee in her film. Li gripped her evening clutch.

"And the Oscar goes to," the host said. Li's heart drummed in her chest.

The cameras trained on her face and on the faces of the four other nominees, projecting them onto a large screen to capture their reactions. Looking at the screen, Li smiled, concealing the tension within.

"Kimberly Adams—*The Red Knife*."

Li felt a bomb fall on her head. But she knew the cameras were still on her, so she smiled and clapped. She felt someone rub her arm. "Are you all right?"

"You'll get it next time."

"Let's go grab a shot after this!"

Her cast and crew were supportive. Li smiled and thanked them. "It's fine," she said. She only prayed her eyes did not reveal the burning inside. She wished her billowing ball gown would swallow her whole.

She became oblivious to everything that followed. There were various performances, banter, and several teary-eyed speeches, but they all washed over Li in a monotonous wave. She wanted nothing more than to go home.

Once the Oscars had ended, Li's cheeks felt sore from smiling all night, in case any cameras were on her. Lian and Mei approached her outside the theatre with sympathetic smiles.

"I'm sorry you didn't win," Mei said. "But it's something extra—you don't need it."

"You will sleep, and tomorrow you will forget all about it," Lian added.

"Let's just go home," Li said.

The limousine journey home was silent. Li stared out the window at the darkness. But the images that popped in her mind were bright and full of color: the life she would now have if she had won that Oscar. More praise. More money. "Academy Award Winner." She'd be in the ranks of the esteemed. The life she should have. The life she deserved.

CHAPTER 26

When Li awoke the next day, she checked her phone on her bedside table; it read 12:00 PM. Immediately, she got up. She grabbed her laptop and flipped it open on her bed. Then she looked herself up online, eager to see how she was being portrayed in the news coverage of the Oscars.

The Oscars Complete List of Winners

...

In the acting category, all eyes were on Shaolina to win Best Supporting Actress. Upsetting expectations, Kimberly Adams won for her performance in *The Red Knife*.

...

Comments (79)

JJ: Shaolina should have won! The Academy are a bunch of racists.

Danggit: The Red Knife was total trash. I walked outta the theatre halfway through the film.

Xo365YV: You are trash Danggit

Paige: Congratulations Kimberly! Well deserved!

Truth Speaker: Shaolina should have won. Shame on you, Academy! You're the ultimate loser for not recognizing real talent when you see it. This is why I no longer watch … See More

Shawn: The Awards are all about politics, not talent.

Li smiled. She might not have won the Oscars, but having the love and support of so many fans was a win in itself.

The Best-Dressed Celebrities on the Oscars Red Carpet

Li clicked on this link. To her delight, she discovered herself on the best-dressed list. She zoomed in on her photo, admiring the contours of her face and the dazzle of her dress against the red carpet.

As she continued searching, a site caught her attention: "Shaolina: Chinese Spy."

Shocked, Li clicked on the link, but it took her to a blank page that read, "Error – Not Found." Her curiosity stoked, Li searched other sites. These had titles like, "Actress Fights Crime Behind the Scenes" or "*Cop Family* Actress Actually Works for FBI." Li was incredulous. *They're just jealous people, spreading rumors. They have nothing better to do with their lives.*

"Shaolina!" her sister's voice called. Mei opened the door and stood in the doorway. A delicious aroma wafted into the room.

"Mom made your favorite foods—even pumpkin pancakes! She kicked the chef out of the kitchen," Mei continued. "For some reason, she doesn't feel comfortable with him around."

Li laughed. "Poor Chef Mario," she said, her eyes still gazing at the screen. "Mom's so used to cooking herself. No wonder she's not comfortable with him." She scrolled down and her face broke into a smile. "There's a picture of you and Mom here from the Oscars. Look!"

"I don't care." Mei grabbed Li's arms and pulled her up. "Let's go eat!"

When Lian placed a bowl of noodles before her a few minutes later, Li slurped it up, savoring every bit. "You make the most delicious food, Mom."

Mei glanced sidelong at her mother, seeking her permission to share something. This time, Lian nodded. "Shaolina, I have some good news to share with you," Mei began. Li looked up from her bowl to find a glimmer of joy in Mei's eyes. "Do you remember the midwife's grandson?"

she said. "He's an elementary school teacher in the village now. Recently, he asked for my hand."

Li gasped and lit up with delight at her sister's news. "Mei, congratulations!" She rose and gave her a tight hug.

"Finally, she got someone," Lian teased. "The poor man doesn't know what he's getting himself into." A chortle escaped her.

"*Mom!*" Mei said.

"You have to prepare for your wedding now!" Li said. She pulled a credit card from her bag and put it in Mei's hand. "You can buy anything you want."

"Won't you come with us?" Mei asked.

"I can't. I have to be at the film set to shoot our new movie. I won't be home for a while." She put a light scarf around her neck, then a crossbody bag.

"Can you tell us more about it?" Mei asked.

"I'm sworn to secrecy and can't tell anyone—especially not you. You have a big mouth." Mei frowned. "I'm just kidding. You and Mom should go to Universal Studios today. You'll enjoy it." Then she dashed out the door.

The next time Li saw them was three days later, over dinner. Mei didn't gobble up her food like before, just picked at it. Lian ate slowly.

"You're not eating." Li's voice filled the silence.

"Remember when father would take us to a restaurant?" Mei sat back in her chair. "It wasn't often, and it wasn't fancy food. But we enjoyed every bite. For months we'd look forward to it. And then for months we'd look back on it. Here, I eat the fanciest food." Mei looked down at her plate of roasted duck and whipped potatoes, garnished with herbs. "But it doesn't bring me the same pleasure."

"Mei, be quiet!" Lian said. "You were licking the plate the first day we came here."

They fell back into silence. Li understood what was really upsetting Mei. They'd traveled thousands of miles, but for the past few days, she'd spent no time with them. But this was her job. Even if she explained to them, they wouldn't understand.

One night, Li managed to arrive home early from set. It was her mother and sister's last day here. The guest bedroom door was ajar. Li pushed it open to find them bent over their luggage, packing. She stepped into the room.

Lian turned to see her and smiled. "Hey, you're back early today." She put her rolled up dress into the bag. Mei shoved her clothes into the bag without looking up.

Li took a step closer. She looked intently at her mother and sister, trying to absorb them with her eyes, trying to memorize their every movement and each detail on their faces.

Suddenly, they were leaving too soon for her. "Stay!" she blurted. "You have nothing back there."

"I can't." Lian shook her head while folding another dress. "I feel lonely here. Back there is home."

Li looked to her sister with pleading eyes. Mei suddenly straightened her back, clasping a bundled-up dress in her hands. "We came all this way for you, but you've spent almost no time with us. And now you're asking us to stay longer? What are we, your entertainment?" She shoved the clothes bundle into the bag and stomped across the cold marble floor towards the window. "You know, when I first came here, I was awed by your marble mansion. But now all I see is cold, dry stone." Placing her hand on the window, she gazed out. "I was wowed by the tiny sparkling city lights below. But now I feel lonely, like I'm isolated from everyone else." During her stay, Mei had realized that everything humans create, no matter how extraordinary at first, eventually becomes ordinary. The only beauty that never expires, that never quenches the appetite, is nature's.

Turning back to Li, she continued, "I guess I actually should thank you for this," she said. "When I was in the village, I was upset that I was poor. I envied the rich because they could buy whatever they wanted, whenever they wanted. But you showed me that being rich past a certain point wouldn't bring me more happiness." She paced towards her handbag and removed the credit card that Li had given her. "Here's your card." She placed it in Li's hand. "Just so you know, we didn't use it."

"Mei!" Lian hissed. "How many times do I have to tell you to watch your mouth?!"

Mei looked up into her sister's eyes. Hurt flickered in them, sending guilt coursing through her. "I'm sorry." Her voice softened. "If this life makes you happy, then I'm happy for you."

The tension in the air between them eased slightly.

"When you finish your movie, come visit us," Lian said. "We'll wait for you, to bury your father's ashes."

A few hours later, Li saw her mother and sister off at the airport. Driving home late that night, with the smooth Hollywood Hills road beneath her tires, she felt a darkness press in on her, as though the night were seeping through her, weighing heavily on her heart. For the next few weeks, she went through her routine as though on autopilot. *Why am I feeling this way? I fulfilled my promise and have so much. I should be the happiest I've ever been.*

She continued to prod her soul one afternoon while driving her Mercedes down the narrow, winding roads to get to the film set. A large, white truck was in front of her. She pressed the brake pedal to slow down. But her car kept speeding towards the truck.

A chill ran up her spine. She pressed again, harder this time. The brake still didn't work. Her heart began to pound now. She pressed the brake and tried the parking brake, but still she was moving closer to the truck. Again, she hit the brakes. And again. The pounding reached her eardrums. A glance to the right revealed a steep, rocky drop. She glanced to the left. She could switch to that lane. Even though her car wouldn't stop, she could avoid imminent collision with the truck ahead. But another car appeared in that lane, blocking her path. She cursed.

As she looked ahead, her eyes were wide with horror. The truck was close. *Too close.* All she could do was honk her horn. So she honked, honked frantically.

Beeeeeeeeeeep.

The sound of her horn reverberated in her head.

It was the last sound she heard before all went black.

CHAPTER 27

Li opened her eyes, only to squint at the bright light above. She waited till her eyes had adjusted. Then she scanned her surroundings: white and pale-blue walls, white tile floors. *Where am I?*

There was something wrapping her head. She felt with her hand—a bandage. Her pulse began to race. *What happened to me?* A memory flickered in her mind. A white truck. A deafening screech. Her breath quickened, and she winced away from the memory. She yearned to turn her head to look around, but she couldn't. Something inhibited her—a neck brace.

With a pounding heart, she glanced sideways only with her eyes now. To her surprise, she saw Aysha. She was on a chair at the bedside, arms crossed, nodding in sleep. *She's supposed to be at college. What is she doing here?*

As Li sat upright, a pang of pain seared through her head. "Ay!" she cried.

Aysha awoke with a start, blinked, and finding Li awake shouted, "Aaah! Girl!" she exhaled. "You almost killed me from worry. Thank God you're alive!" She stood up and leaned over her friend.

"What happened?" Li asked.

"I got a call from the hospital that you were in a car accident. I flew back immediately."

A knock on the door sounded, and a doctor entered. He was in his mid-fifties with thinning gray hair. "Good morning," he said. He checked Li's pulse and asked, "How are you doing?"

"My neck hurts."

He nodded. "You've had a mild cervical dislocation." Li's face went pale. He took a file from a clipboard at the front of Li's bed, scribbled something on it, and said, "It could have been much worse. You could have damaged your spinal cord and been paralyzed."

Aysha gasped and grabbed Li's arm, looking at the doctor intently. "Will she be okay now?"

He nodded and turned to Li. "After a few days, we can start physiotherapy. Hopefully, you'll be better in a few weeks. Meanwhile, I'll prescribe you an anti-inflammatory and some pain medication."

They thanked the doctor, who then left.

Li was released from the hospital a few days later, and Aysha stayed to look after her. Meanwhile, police began investigations of the incident.

Li was in bed one afternoon when Aysha's voice sounded from behind the door. "Knock, knock," she sang. Aysha gently pushed the door with her hip, then entered carrying a tray with a bowl.

"I made you bone broth!" she said cheerily. "It's good for healing your ligaments and joints!"

Li sat up in bed, grateful that she had someone who cared for her. "Thank you." She accepted the tray.

Aysha sat in the chair beside her. As Li raised the spoon to her lips, Aysha eyed her, making sure her friend drank up. Then she sat back. "So have you told your family about the accident?"

"No need," Li replied, between sips. "I'm fine, I don't need to worry them." Aysha nodded slowly. "You should also return to college." Li looked at her. "I think I'm already feeling the healing effects of your broth."

Aysha smiled. Eight days after the accident, she returned to her studies at college.

The police investigated and soon figured out it hadn't been an accident; someone had tampered with her brake lines. They interrogated everyone working for her, from her security guard and gardener to her cleaning lady and chef. But the culprit was yet to be determined.

They warned Li to take extra precautions. Someone wanted her dead. She was baffled. What had she ever done to harm anyone? Sure, there were always jealous people, even haters, but who'd actually try to kill her?

While the incident had endangered her life, it enhanced her livelihood. Celebrity magazines and news networks covered the chilling incident, and a myriad of celebrities and fans sent her supportive, loving messages.

After a few weeks, Li could remove her neck brace. But the pain in her neck nagged and held her back.

Her prescribed opioids were insufficient to ease her pain, and her doctor had to give her higher doses.

She tried returning to her daily exercise routine. But things that had been simple suddenly became insurmountable. *I ran up and down mountains every day! Why can't I run across this flat field?* she rebuked herself through teary eyes and clenched teeth. Her Shaolin training had been the one constant in her turbulent life, keeping her grounded. It had always helped her shake off her anger and draining thoughts. Sweat, not tears, was her catharsis. When she had walked the streets, it was what threw her shoulders back and her head up. It was what gave her the confidence and courage to take on whatever came her way, to meet the world eye to eye. It was a core part of her identity. So when it was gone, she wasn't sure of herself anymore.

Slowly, her body began losing its shape. Maybe others had yet to notice, but she felt her lean armor of muscle melt, turning her into a regular person. Except she lacked another strong skill set to distinguish her. It upset her.

She missed when her body could do almost anything her mind willed it to. She missed when she could leap into the air on command and take down foes. A gap was growing between what she could do and what she yearned to do. It made her feel weaker, detached from physical self. Her body was no longer "her." It became but a vehicle, carrying her head. Increasingly unable to live with her body, she began to live in her head.

Li's next movie, *Black Mountain*, featured many action-packed scenes in nature, from climbing mountains to jumping off cliffs. Most of its actors would rely on stunt doubles—but not Li, who was famous for performing her own stunts. She wasn't about to tarnish that reputation.

Filming of the action scenes began two months after her incident and required her to parachute off a soaring helicopter. So she found herself standing there, 14,000 feet in the air, deafening blades above. In her jumpsuit, she put on her headgear and goggles. As her two assistants triple-checked the harness, cinching it tightly, a lightening pain shot up the back of her head. She winced and squeezed her neck.

"Are you okay?" one assistant shouted.

Li gave a thumbs-up. Then she stood at the edge of the open door. Gazing down, thousands of feet from the ground, she saw mostly green earth, with a few brown patches. The height didn't scare her. As a warrior monk, she was used to being up high mountains and on cliff edges. The assistants then helped her put on her parachute backpack. This time, the lightening pain she felt was more acute. "Ay!" she cried.

"Are you sure you're okay?" the assistant shouted. She did not respond this time, so the assistant grabbed his radio transmitter, which connected him to the producer, and said, "Sir, she's in a lot of pain. I think she's unfit to perform the stunt."

There was a moment of silence on the transmitter, then, "Okay, come back down."

When the chopper landed, the director angrily marched towards it.

"*What happened?*" he yelled.

"Sir, she appears to have severe neck pain," the assistant replied. Li was about to protest but knew he was right. "Safety is our priority," the assistant continued.

With his hands on his hips, the director looked away and exhaled impatiently. "We don't have *time* for this!" he yelled. They needed to shoot the scene in daylight and while the sky was clear and the winds just right.

"Okay, let's just get a stunt double to do it," he said finally and marched off.

Li looked down, feeling herself shrink. This was the first time she had not been able to perform a stunt. She felt worthless.

Soon, her stunt double, Mia, arrived on set. Mia was a light-skinned African American in her early thirties who had been in the army and was often called on for military scenes.

Li watched on the sidelines as Mia quickly got briefed on the scene, then hopped into the helicopter.

"Let's roll," the director spoke through his radio transmitter once the helicopter was in position.

Thousands of feet up in the air, the stunt double jumped, and everyone on the ground gazed upward.

For a few seconds, they couldn't see anything. Then a tiny black dot appeared.

Li was sitting, drinking from her water bottle while she watched the single black dot tumble closer to them.

Suddenly, her eyes opened wide in horror. *Something's wrong.* She sprang from her seat and dropped the bottle to the ground. There was only the stunt double falling with her parachute backpack. No parachute canopy billowed over her yet.

"Why isn't she opening her parachute?" the director cried.

"She's crazy!" a crewmember yelled. "Open the parachute!"

All the crewmembers got to their feet, their stomachs freefalling along with the stunt double. "Open the parachute!" they cried. "Open the frickin' parachute!!!"

As the stunt double got closer to earth, they could see that she was trying, pulling frantically on the cords.

"*COME ON!*" the crewmembers cried in despair.

She pulled. Again and again. But the parachute wouldn't open. They could see the panic on her face.

Everyone on the ground was paralyzed in fear, their jaws frozen open and their breath held as they witnessed the stunt double tumble down like a rock, then strike the ground, raising a cloud of dust on impact.

For a moment, everyone froze. The only movement was the beating of their hearts.

Then the paramedics rushed before them, to the fallen stunt double. It didn't take long before they turned to the crew and declared the inevitable.

A wave of sorrow inundated them.

In the ensuing investigation, police found that someone had tampered with the parachute—which clearly had originally been meant for Li.

With this attempt following only two months after the brake incident, Li was compelled to ramp up security around her mansion, and she hired guards to follow her in public.

But more than fear, what ate away at her was guilt. *She* had been the target of murder, but another woman had died instead. Because of her. She had unknowingly sacrificed herself for Li. But Li still couldn't understand who wanted to kill her or why.

CHAPTER 28

Monks used their realization that death was an inevitable part of life to live more fully. But Li now felt like she was in a shadow life. Every sound sent her into panic. At night, she couldn't sleep. It was as though a blade were hanging over her head, about to fall any second.

Her constant tension only exacerbated her neck pain. When she awoke, she wasn't in control of how her day would go. It depended on her level of pain. Some days, it was manageable. But others, it was acute, freezing her in place and radiating to her shoulders and arms. As she dialed down her training, she became uncertain how to fill her day and create a new routine. When she looked at her softening body in the mirror, hot tears stung her eyes. Increasingly, a stranger stared back.

But to the public, she had to remain the warrior, if not in personality then in pretense. Her fan base expected it. So she popped more pain pills and donned a warrior's mask, plastering on a smile and praying her eyes would not betray her.

For the first time, she was timid. Fear dominated her psyche. When people addressed her, she avoided eye contact, afraid they'd see the weakness within. She fidgeted, worried they'd judge her negatively. She no longer knew how to respond. With a core part of her identity missing, she felt spineless. She could play any character but had no character of her own. Uncertainty and second-guesses marked everything she said. The paparazzi snapping photos of her, and reporters making permanent every word she uttered only accentuated this. Her anxiety-riddled thoughts became her constant companions.

Unable to channel her pain, she was soon drawn into a whirlpool of depression. Food had no flavor, scenery had no color, and sleep was devoid of dreams. Even her laughter was mirthless. Hollow within, she was like a black hole, consuming all light and wanting everything. Nothing was enough for her. Yet simultaneously, she was not enough for anything.

To ease her physical and emotional pain, she took more prescription drugs. One night, standing on her patio, she was in the trenches of another drug craving. She looked out at the dark canvas of the sky, the silhouette of black hills. The urge to cry was overwhelming. Her life was just a leap from one peak to another. She could always get another drink, another dose, another paycheck, another high. But the pleasure from them was ephemeral. What was the point of refilling her glass when she knew it would empty, that after a brief high she would fall low again?

Some saw the glass half full and others saw it half empty. But she saw a hole in her cup. Regardless of how much she had, she couldn't hold onto the pleasures of life. When everything was dull, what was the point in anything?

CHAPTER 29

It was an early summer evening when Aysha returned from college to visit Li. They were sitting around the dinner table as the chef came to place dazzling dishes before them.

Aysha looked at her gold-rimmed plate, carrying ribeye steak drizzled in sauce and surrounded by peas. She took a bite, chewing the food fully and savoring the flavors.

Picking up her fork, Li tried to stab a pea on her plate. It evaded her. She chased it with her fork. Again it rolled away.

Clang!

Aysha looked up to find that Li had dropped her fork on the plate and pulled a packet of cigarettes from her handbag. Her hands were trembling as she lit a cigarette and raised it to her cracked lips. She took a drag and exhaled.

Aysha gazed at Li's face. The skin beneath her eyes was dark and sagging. Even the dim dining hall light and her mask of makeup could not conceal her paleness. A gaunt face peered out between curtains of long, dark, thin hair. Everything about her face, from the bags under her eyes to the corners of her mouth, was drawn downward. Sadness gripped Aysha's heart. "I didn't know you smoked," she said.

"Do you have a problem with that?" Li snapped.

"No," Aysha said slowly. "How are you doing? Really?"

In Aysha, Li had a confidante, someone with whom she could speak aloud the complaints that festered in her mind. She pressed the stub of her cigarette onto her plate, then kept hold of it. "I can't sleep," she said. She shrugged. "I can't *not* feel pain constantly throbbing in my body. I can't not have these—these *thoughts* that something bad is going to happen. That—that—I can't get a *break* from them!" She wiggled the cigarette harder onto the plate. "I don't know what happy feels like anymore." Her voice broke into a squeak, and thick tears flooded her eyes. "I just feel so sad, Aysha, and I don't know *why*."

A moment of silence passed as Aysha absorbed and thought about her friend's words. "You've been working really hard," she finally said. "I think you're tired. You need a break. You need a vacation."

"Yeah," Li exhaled heavily, finally letting go of the cigarette stub. "I'm thinking of visiting my family in China, once I finish shooting this stupid film." She sighed.

"You know," Aysha said in a cheery voice, "when I tell my friends at school that we're friends, they don't believe me. They say, 'No way, you're friends with that superstar?' I have to show them *photos* of us together!" Li smiled.

The chef approached, carrying a tray of drinks. They each took one. Aysha raised her glass. "Let's forget all this. The past is behind us. Here's to a brighter future."

They clinked glasses, and Li took a gulp. That was her last memory. Then she was consumed by darkness.

CHAPTER 30

Li groaned and her head ached as she slowly opened her eyes. All around her was a hazy darkness. *Is this real?* The air was hot and uncomfortable, and she was sweating. Slowly, her eyes adjusted, allowing her to take in her surroundings.

Shards of glinting glass and metal scraps littered a concrete floor. She looked up and around. It was a massive open space, two stories high. And windows, some broken, lined the walls, revealing a glowing moon and black night sky.

Boooooo-oooooom. A foghorn sounded in the distance, shaking away the vestiges of her drowsiness.

This seemed to be an abandoned warehouse by the harbor, and she was in the center of it. Chained to a metal chair. Her heart pounded. *Where am I? How did I get here?* She struggled against her chains, but they wouldn't budge. Gritting her teeth, she pulled against the chains again. Still nothing. Her breathing quickened and panic flooded her system. *Why am I here?* A feral rage rose in her at being trapped here without reason. She screamed, then tried once more to pull herself free. It was no use.

Suddenly, a door clicked in the distance. Her breath caught. Far across from her, the warehouse door squealed open, and two men with flashlights stepped to each side of the door. Li strained her eyes. From between them, the silhouette of a massive man emerged.

Her pulse accelerated as she saw him. He was broad shouldered, with narrow hips and long legs. He said something to the men, who went out and closed the door behind them. Then he began to move towards her, directing the flashlight at her face. She squinted and could tell he was approaching from the intensity of the light and the sound of his thick-soled boots.

He stepped closer and closer, until he stood right before her.

Li lifted her gaze to his face. Her heart leapt to her throat, stifling another scream. She wanted to look away but couldn't, paralyzed by fear.

Half his face was burned.

As the skin over his right eye socket was sealed shut, he stared at her with his left, obsidian eye. The hairs on her arms rose.

"Shaolina," he boomed, his voice laced with temper. "Finally, I get to meet you."

"Who are you?" she snapped. "And why am I here?"

He paused and looked at her. His iron eye seemed to bore into her. "They call me Robin."

The name was somehow familiar to Li, tugging at a distant memory.

"I was a soldier," he said. "For three years, I was deployed abroad. Then one day, I watched a bomb blow my friend to pieces." As he said those last words, there was an explosion of fire in his eye. He faced her, but Li knew his mind was back at that scene.

"I—." His breathing became heavy. "I froze." His voice was a rasp now. "As the fire engulfed my best friend, then burned half of me. When I returned to America, Veterans Affairs was useless. They did the bare minimum. Many of my friends didn't die on the front line, they died in the waiting line—waiting for help, committing suicide or drinking or drugging themselves to death because they couldn't live with the trauma, the horror. When I looked for work, nobody would hire me. They didn't see the fire I'd survived on duty. All they saw was my burnt face."

He paced. The light from his torch fell away from Li's eyes, giving her some respite.

"Every day, *every single day*, I drowned in unbearable pain," he continued. "Pain that nothing could numb. But instead of helping me, people called me insane. And there are thousands of vets like me." He thought of the soldiers who sacrificed their health only to be denied their health benefits, who worked hard only to come back unemployed, who protected the home front only to become homeless. "We give everything, then when we're used up, damaged goods, we're burdens on the system and get chucked away."

Li's memory flickered back to her village. She gazed out vacantly as her mind filled with scenes of her uncle's smashed plate on the floor, how he had compared it to her father. It had served him all those years, but once broken, it was useless.

"I'm sorry." She spoke as though to someone else. The man looked at her. "I'm sorry." The shards of glass on the concrete floor now glinted more visibly, bringing her back to the warehouse. "I'm sorry for what happened to you," she said softly. "I—"

"Tell me who you're working for," he snapped.

Li frowned. "What do you mean? I'm an actress. I work with different directors."

"Wrong answer." Without warning, he threw a punch to her face. The force of it knocked her chair back, slamming her skull against the floor. Pain coursed through her head and neck. She felt blood trickling from her nose, down toward her ear.

Her breathing accelerated. This was real. There was no director to call "Cut!" and end the horror scene. There was only her and this tormentor, and she didn't know how it would end.

As he lifted her chair back up, her head throbbed. "Remember when you caught my men at the bank?" Li nodded. "Me and my men took money from the banks and gave it to veterans and their families. I'm sure somewhere in your Shaolin training, they taught you something about balance. I was trying to address this imbalance between rich and poor. Everything was going well. Until you interfered."

He narrowed his eye at her. "Not only did you catch my men, but you and your team interfered when we tried to hack the banks' computers."

Li could only stare in disbelief. The air was densely humid, making breathing difficult. "I did stop a bank robbery, but the hacking?! I don't know what you're talking about. I have no idea how to hack or to stop hackers."

He gave a short, humorless laugh. "For years, you lied to everyone that you were a boy. But you can't deceive me."

Li was shocked. No one outside her village knew that she'd disguised herself as a boy. "How did you—"

"How much do you pay your chef, Mario?" he said, grinning.

Alarm thrummed through Li's veins. She remembered her mother's discomfort about Mario being around, watching them, listening to their conversations. She remembered the drink he'd served her, the last memory she had before waking up here.

"Apparently, you don't pay him enough, because he told me everything," he continued. "He told me that during the three days when you left your family back at the mansion, our hacking plan was foiled and we lost millions."

"*What?* That's just a coincidence! I was away shooting a film!"

The man jutted his jaw forward, about to throw another blow, but one of his guards entered. "Boss, the other girl is screaming and causing trouble."

Aysha! Li thought.

"Bring her in," said Robin.

The guard nodded and exited, returning half a minute later with his partner. Between them, they pulled a handcuffed woman.

"Aysha!" Li shouted.

"Shaolina!" Aysha cried, gasping at Li's bloody face. She attempted to run to Li, but the guards held her back. "Why are we here?!" she yelled. "What do they want from us?"

At the sound of Aysha's voice, Robin had frozen. He turned to her and said, *"Aysha?* Is that really you? Joshua's sister?"

Aysha peered at him. Despite the dim light and burn scars, she recognized him. "Tyler?"

His mouth opened in shock.

Aysha gasped. It was him, her brother's best friend. They'd been deployed together before her brother was killed. She said, "Tyler what's happening? Why are we here? Why are you doing this to me and Shaolina?"

Tyler stared down at Li. "It's because of her!"

"What?" Aysha exclaimed. "She's never done anything, not a single thing, except help me. She lifted me from the streets and gave me a new life."

Tyler looked back at Aysha. "She may have saved your life, but she ruined the lives of many more people. I was going to use you to make her talk. But out of respect for your brother's soul, I'll let you go."

"Please, don't hurt her," Aysha pleaded.

He gave a nod to his men, who began pulling Aysha toward the door. Aysha screamed, fighting their grasp. *"Please!"*

"Enough!" Tyler yelled. "I don't have time for your dramatics." He eyed Aysha being dragged out, then drew a gun from inside his jacket and pressed it to Li's head. "I'll give you two options," he snarled. "Either you tell me which group you work for and what they know about us, or you die. I'm going to count to three."

Panic overwhelmed Li. She could not think.

"One."

She was not supposed to be here. This man was mistaken, and he was going to kill her. Fury boiled up in her, rage that in a fraction of a second, someone could take her life, after everything she had worked for and all that she had, as if her life was worthless. And anger that there was nothing she could do.

But just as quickly as it had come, her storm of anger and frustration dissolved. The fog in her mind cleared, revealing what was most important. On this journey between birth and death, she had strayed, gotten lost, and lost sight of the essentials. Now that she saw them again, she felt as though an ocean were deluging the chambers of her heart, drowning her. She was sinking to the bottom. She gasped, she fought, she tried to surface. *If only I could*—. But like stinging saltwater, regret clawed up the back of her throat, choking her. She was not ready to die. Tears streamed down her cheeks, as though the salt in her throat had found an outlet through her eyes. But weeping couldn't drain the ocean inside.

"Two."

If only she could turn back time. She would know how to live and what to do.

"Three."

Her time was up. She squeezed her eyes shut, tears streaming down her face. *Goodbye, Mother. Goodbye, Mei.* Feeling like a filthy bag that needed to be thrown away, she surrendered herself to death.

Boom.

A loud gunshot reverberated, rattling the warehouse windows.

But Li felt no pain. *Is this what death is like?* She wasn't supposed to escape the darkness of her closed lids. Yet slowly, miraculously, she managed to open her eyes. She still had control over the switch between darkness and light.

That's when she saw him beside her: Tyler was on the floor, gripping his bleeding hand. Someone from a window above had shot the hand holding the gun.

"YOU'RE UNDER ARREST!" a voice called through a megaphone.

A swarm of policemen burst through the door, filling the warehouse like a navy-colored sea. They surrounded Tyler.

Looking around at them, Li finally felt secure. All the weight of anger and fear that she'd been carrying over the years now seemed palpable; her body felt weak and ready to collapse. She had no more energy to be angry, to be anxious, to be afraid. She had energy just to be. So she closed her eyes and let herself rest.

She could hear sounds around her and feel people approach. She was freed from the chair, then lifted onto a stretcher, and an oxygen mask was placed on her face. She felt as though she was floating on air. At that moment, she knew her wish had been granted. This was her second chance.

CHAPTER 31

"Elusive Gang Leader Finally Caught"

LOS ANGELES – The hunt for one of California's most elusive gang leaders came to an end yesterday. Thirty-eight-year-old Tyler Powell was holding two people captive in an abandoned warehouse when police swooped in to arrest him. He was charged with organized crime, drug trafficking, kidnapping, assault, and several other offences.

LA's police chief praised the department's remarkable feat. Police had begun tracking the gang leader after investigations revealed a link between a series of bank robberies that have swept California in recent years. But the shadowy leader remained elusive, known on the streets only by his alias, Robin. With Robin's arrest, the Hoods gang has "practically been dismantled," in the words of Police Chief Gregory Hill.

How a Hollywood Actress Was Caught in the Quagmire

One of Powell's two captives yesterday was Hollywood actress Shaolina. Her abduction was the culmination of attempts on her life since March. Four years ago, Shaolina had stopped a bank robbery, then indirectly helped stop several more through her role as a bank security guard training manager. Enhanced security training and banks' overall shift towards an online platform have made physical bank robberies more difficult and less lucrative, so the Hoods gang moved to hacking banks. After a couple of successful hacks, though, they were stymied by the banks adopting enhanced cyber security. It's believed that Powell thought Shaolina was responsible for this, since tabloids and online rumors have portrayed the actress as continuing to play an active but behind-the-scenes role in protecting the banks.

The source of these rumors and false news items has yet to be determined, but several theories are already circulating. Some claim the FBI were using Shaolina as bait to catch the elusive gang leader. Her celebrity status helped the rumors spread, and her past security job made them more credible, they state. Others suggest a rival gang rather than the FBI were behind the plan. The gang leader's resulting capture of the celebrity—heavily tracked by paparazzi—would lead the police to capture him, eliminating him from the turf battles between the rival gangs.

Neither theory has been substantiated. It's also possible there was no single source. "Fanned by the entertainment media, rumors can take on a life of their own," one commentator noted, "and become life-threatening."

Li felt there were larger forces behind this. It was unlikely she'd find out, and she didn't want to waste her time on vengeance. She needed time away to reflect on her life. Finishing up the film, she liquidated her material assets—cars, clothing, jewelry, mansion, the whole lot—then donated much of the money, supporting students' educations, orphans, the homeless, as well as veterans and their families. She also gave a sum to Aysha. She realized that the greatest thing money could buy was the ability to give more.

CHAPTER 32

Autumn, China

The sun had not yet risen, and Lian was in bed, under her quilt. The autumn winds howled through the house, and from the room nearby, she could hear Mei's snoring. It had been a while since they'd received a letter from Li. She hoped her daughter was okay. *Probably just too busy to write*, she reassured herself.

Knock, knock, knock. She opened her eyes. Was it a tree branch tapping on their rooftop? The wind howled. Yes, it probably was. No one would be knocking at this hour. She closed her eyes.

Knock, knock, knock. Again, the sound came. Heart thumping, Lian rose to her feet, afraid of what person or news would be coming so early. She wrapped her shawl around her tightly and picked up a lantern, then walked to the door, her heart seeming to beat faster with every step.

As she opened the door, the dim light of her lantern revealed a bony face with sharp, shadowy edges. It was like she was staring at the apparition of her husband. The lantern in her hand trembled. When she blinked and looked again, she realized it was Li. She had tied her hair back and was wearing brown garments.

"*Shaolina!* Is that you?!" As the figure nodded, Lian took Li's hand and gently drew her inside.

Rapid footsteps approached from behind. Mei also had awoken at the knocking, then had leapt out of bed upon hearing her sister's name. "Shaolina! You're here!" She rushed forward and enveloped her sister in a tight embrace. Then she looked at her incredulously before inundating her with questions. "Why haven't you replied to our letters? Why didn't you tell us you were coming? How are you doing?"

Li opened her mouth to answer but didn't know what to say. "I'm tired, I'm tired," she said slowly, looking at her mother.

Lian too was burning with questions for Li but realized she was in no condition to answer. "Mei, stop it," she said. "Go get her some of your comfortable clothes, and let her sleep in her bed." Mei rushed to a cabinet to pull out her softest clothing.

"It's okay, it will be okay," Lian said softly to Li. "Now you can rest."

Li gratefully slipped on Mei's clothes, then got into the bed, and Mei tucked her in, then let her be.

Li felt the soft fabric of her clothing against her skin. Her mother had sewed it using flour sacks. The weighty quilt seemed to embrace her body and alleviate the aching and fatigue. Even the wind, howling through the roof, circulated fresh air throughout the house. Its cries melded with the whispers of her mother and sister from the next room. Li took a deep breath. As her eyes closed, a gentle smile appeared on her face. She slid into a peaceful slumber.

When she opened her eyes again, she could see golden rays shining through the small window. A rooster's calls outside pierced the air, and the howling wind had stopped. She stretched, then removed the quilt. As her bare feet touched the wooden floor, she was surprised at how light and satisfied her body felt. Her soul felt snug in her body. All around her arms, she felt the flow of a joyous currency. She had slept for only an hour or so, but rest had worked wonders.

As she entered the living room, she was met by a delicious aroma and found her mother stirring warm rice porridge while Mei set the table.

"Finally, you're awake!" Mei beamed while arranging cups. "You slept for a whole day!"

This caught Li by surprise. She seated herself at the table, and as her mother set down a bowl, her stomach gurgled. It had been a while since she'd felt hungry, truly hungry. Grabbing the warm bowl with both hands, she took a slurp. It was soothing and delicious. She took another slurp, absorbed in her rice porridge. Meanwhile, Mei stared at her, eager for an opportunity to ask questions. But their mother frowned and gave a slight shake of the head.

Finally, Li finished her meal and sat back. She was ready to tell them what had happened.

She had left not because she had everything, but because she had enough, and she'd had enough. The brilliance of gold and the spotlight of fame had been so bright that she'd been blinded. So bright that everything else had seemed dark and lifeless. Everything else around her had faded from sight. She could appreciate little else besides the money and fame. They had granted her so much that, in the end, she took so much for granted.

She related what had happened since their departure, from her accidents to her encounter with Robin and his gang, and how she now felt spent and exhausted. She shared her disenchantment with the material world and told them about selling her possessions and donating most of the resulting money. She opened up about her addiction to drugs and alcohol, and her desire to restart her life.

Lian and Mei both grew quiet, amazed by all that had transpired. Mei looked down at her lap, forehead furrowed in consternation. As Li looked to her mother, she saw tears in the older woman's eyes. Lian suddenly grasped Li's hand on the table, grateful her daughter was alive and here with her.

"We will help you," Lian said. "With your will power and our support, you can heal from your pain and troubles. We won't leave you alone again."

They sat in silence.

"Remember when you gave us money to build ourselves a new house?" Mei finally spoke.

Li nodded slowly.

"We decided to save it for you. Since I'm getting married, I won't be living here anymore."

"And I'm not leaving this house," Lian added. "It contains too many precious memories of your father."

"Speaking of father," Mei said, "Now that you're here, we can bury his ashes in our land."

Lian nodded. "We should invite your uncle."

After breakfast, Li walked to her uncle's house. On the way, she took in the surrounding scenery. Several roosters crowed from atop villagers' homes. Two men working in the fields paused and looked at her. "Who's that?" one asked. "The face looks familiar."

"I think that's Shaolina!" the other said.

An older woman was carrying a basket with vegetables and walking along the dirt path. She looked closely and exclaimed, "Yes! It's Shaolina!"

But in rapt contemplation of the fields, Li scarcely felt their voices wash over her. She kept walking, and her uncle's house was soon before her. The red main gates were slightly ajar. As she pushed through, their hinges squealed in protest. It was the only sound. There was no swelling laughter or cacophony of conversation. No crowd congregated in the courtyard. The only guests here were dead leaves scattered on the ground, and these were beginning to decay, merging into the brown dirt.

The large cage that once had held motley-colored birds was now empty, save for a few feathers and droppings on the bottom of the cage.

Li stepped into the center of the courtyard, where the fountain had once hosted golden koi. Now, it was dry, inhabited only by more dead leaves. A soft breeze caressed her nose. When she lifted her gaze in its direction, she saw him.

In a corner, with his back to her, was her uncle. He was sitting in a wheelchair, tossing breadcrumbs to birds who hopped around his feet.

"Uncle," she called.

The man stiffened. He then slowly wheeled his chair around to face her. Li's mouth opened slightly as she saw how he had aged. Sunken eyes gazed from a pallid face. His skin was heavily lined. His once rotund body was now a light collection of meager flesh and jutting bones.

"Shaolina?" His voice was a mixture of surprise and sadness.

"Yes, Uncle, it's me—your brother's daughter."

"I've heard a lot about you. What brings you here?"

"I came to invite you to my father's ceremony. We are burying his ashes in our family land."

He looked away, unable to bring himself to meet her eyes. "Thank you for inviting me... after... everything..." He swallowed with evident difficulty. "I will attend."

Still avoiding direct eye contact, his eyes slid to the corner where he had smashed his plate and compared its broken pieces to her father. He cringed internally at the memory.

Li, too, looked at that corner.

"Sometimes..." His voice was a rasp as he tried to speak again. "Sometimes, we step on the sand, thinking we will always stand above it." He shook his head. "We never anticipate the day we will sink beneath it. And at that moment, guilt engulfs us, guilt that we were not better human beings, guilt that we didn't give when we could. But that realization comes too late. Because once we sink to the bottom of the sand, we have nothing left to give." He kept his watery gaze on that corner, while a tangle of emotions encircled his throat.

"Uncle," Li stepped forward, "it's not too late for you. As long as you have breath in your body, you have something to give." She looked down at his frail, freckled hands holding the bread. "Even if it's giving breadcrumbs to tiny birds."

He spoke not a word, just swallowed again and threw another crumb.

Li let him be.

CHAPTER 33

After her father's ceremony, Li strolled to the walnut tree that had sheltered her father when he took breaks from work. She sat on the grass and fallen yellow leaves beneath the tree's canopy, then took a deep breath, satisfied that she had fulfilled her promise to her father's memory.

Up ahead was the path that led to the Shaolin Temple. She thought of her shifu and the brother monks. She missed them. She would visit them, but not before she first strengthened her mind and body.

She then gazed ahead at a series of white clouds traversing the sky, each seeming to have its own destination. All had their duty: to bring rainfall. She looked down to the earth, at a line of ants carrying scraps of food, each contributing to the collective bounty. She listened to the buzz of the bees in the fields, each pollinating the crops. She felt her back in contact with the bark of the tree. These trees were shade and shelter in a summer's swelter and an autumn's pelter. She remembered her shifu's teachings: everything in nature was connected to a larger purpose, and to an ecosystem and a community. She reflected on her own life. It was when she had become disconnected, when she felt uptight with others, when she was locked up in her head, when her dreams had become so lofty that she forgot her roots to the earth—that's when her life had lost its meaning.

Those past years, she had lost her inner tranquility. But, when she thought about it, nature wasn't always tranquil. In the air, tornadoes emerged. In the water, tsunamis arose. With fire, volcanoes erupted. And on land, earthquakes unfolded. Yet after a bout of tumult, calm returned. It was natural to experience unrest and uncertainty. But now that she had received this second chance, what would she do?

She looked down at the ruby ring on her finger, at the depth of its blazing red gem. She thought of the pressures this rock had gone through to become a ruby. Then she closed her eyes. A breeze brushed against her face as she ruminated, and she let herself breathe deeply. When she opened her eyes again, she smiled. She knew what she was going to do.

CHAPTER 34

Many years later

Li breathed in the fragrance of jasmine and osmanthus that filled the fresh air. Dawn was painting the sky pink, and Li was watering her garden. Tree peonies, azaleas, and other delicate flowers bloomed, their soft petals cradling droplets of morning dew. She was in her orange robes, and her hair was tied back in a ponytail. So many birds were singing, each to their own melody, yet together forming a synchronized harmony. Dragonflies floated about the plants, and in the emerging sunlight, their wings glinted colorfully. This place was so alive that it filled her with life.

"Shifu," a girl's voice called. She turned to see her twelve-year-old student running up to her.

Li had decided to build a Shaolin school for boys and girls from around the world on her family land. She smiled at her student.

"There is mail for you." The student handed her a

large, padded envelope. Li thanked her, and the girl ran back to her training.

From time to time, Aysha would send Li letters. But this time, the envelope was heavier than expected. *What could it be?* Li wondered.

She settled on a smooth, cool rock overlooking a small ravine where a lively stream burbled. All around her, the morning dew flowed and dragonflies danced. She tore open the package and first pulled out a smaller envelope, which contained a single sheet of paper:

Hi, girl!

How are you? Hope you're doing great!

Now brace yourself, because I have some news to share…

I got engaged! Yes, you read that right. I met my fiancé in senior year of college, and I can't wait for this new chapter in our lives.

Shaolina, through our years together, you've taught me so much. You've given me a family when I had none. You've supported me so I could gain the most valuable tool to support myself: education. I wanted to share the lessons I learned from you with others. So I did something about it…

Li was baffled by the last sentence. *What did she do?* Something heavy remained in the padded envelope. Drawing it out, she found a giftwrapped book. When she unwrapped it and read the title, a smile spread across her face.

"SHAOLINA"

ABOUT THE AUTHOR

Maha Al Fahim graduated with the highest honors in Public Policy from Princeton University. She is currently pursuing her Master's in International Policy at Stanford University.

Made in the USA
Middletown, DE
24 October 2020